D1362689

"Four in the Morning?"

How dare he wake her at this hour after she'd said she wouldn't go! "Bart Hall, I told you—"

"But I told the boys that you were an expert fisherwoman!" Leanne heard a muffled sound that she recognized as giggles. Bart moved aside and the light revealed two small figures in the shadows. He must have figured out that she was a pushover for children. It was a dirty trick, and she'd have to figure out a way to get even, but for now, it seemed she was going fishing.

Dear Reader:

In times like these more and more people are turning to their faith. And they want to read about people like themselves, people who hold the same beliefs dear. If this sounds familiar, you might find that SILHOUETTE INSPIRATIONS are about people like you.

SILHOUETTE INSPIRATIONS are love stories with a difference—they are novels of hope and faith about people who have made a commitment or recommitment of their lives to Christ. And SILHOUETTE INSPIRATIONS are also wonderful romances about men and women experiencing all the joy of falling in love—romances that will touch your heart.

SILHOUETTE INSPIRATIONS—more than just a love story, a love story you'll cherish!

The Editors
SILHOUETTE INSPIRATIONS

A QUESTION OF TRUST
Shelia Shook

Silhouette Inspirations

Published by Silhouette Books New York

America's Publisher of Contemporary Romance

SILHOUETTE BOOKS, a Division of Simon & Schuster, Inc.
1230 Avenue of the Americas, New York, N.Y. 10020

Distributed by Pocket Books

ISBN: 0-671-45291-6

First Silhouette Books printing July, 1984

10 9 8 7 6 5 4 3 2 1

America's Publisher of Contemporary Romance

Printed in the U.S.A.

A QUESTION OF TRUST

Chapter One

Leanne watched the water ripple as she dropped her fishing line in again. The slow-moving water gently carried the float downstream. She had been fishing for over an hour and had caught nothing. A gentle breeze teased at her long dark-brown hair, sending loose strands to tickle her face. She stretched her slender legs onto a rock slab at the edge of the water and watched the evening fall on the wooded area across the narrow stream. It was wonderful to have the babbling water at her own back door.

This little plot of land was the best birthday gift her father could have given her, though she hadn't thought so at the time. But that had been nearly two years ago, and at the age of twenty-one she had had other things on her mind—like Eric Davenport, the handsome buyer from New York. What a fool she had been to fall for him. He had only wanted one thing from her and had stayed around for two years determined she would give in to him. He had had her convinced of his love, and she had thought she loved him, too, when she agreed to marry him. Then, after one of his many trips to New York, he just didn't come back. Later, she was crushed to find out that he had also been engaged to another woman during the last few months of their relationship.

Closing her eyes, Leanne let her head fall back so that her tanned face was exposed to the gentle breeze whispering through her long hair. The fresh smell of pine filled the air and she felt a chill go up her spine. She opened her eyes to the melon colors of the Oklahoma sky and watched a bird coast lazily, then flap his wings and disappear behind the dark edge of the treetops. She was glad she had decided to move out of the city. She felt a closeness to God out here. Having lived most of her life in the country, she had missed it and was now glad to be back. Tulsa was a growing city and its fast pace was enough for her to contend with when she went in to work. At least now she could spend her evenings and weekends away from the sound of horns and sirens. Her move had disappointed her father a little, though. "How do you expect to make me a grandfather if you move yourself out here in the sticks?" he had said. "Not that I don't want you closer to home, but who's gonna come way out here? And don't tell me Stephen Carlile, either! That young man isn't worth his salt. Inherited his money, he did. Didn't work a day in his life."

Leanne smiled as she thought of her father's thin, red-skinned face, weathered by years of working in the hot sun at the Delta oil wells. He wanted a grandson to take the place of the son he never had, and was always bringing home some young man for her to meet. But it would be a long time before she would get seriously involved with anyone again. Stephen was fun to be with, and right now that was enough for her. Nevertheless, her father kept telling her that love was like riding a horse: "If you fall off, you have to get right back on."

"Well, I never was much for horses," Leanne would say, laughing halfheartedly; one heartbreak in a lifetime was enough for her.

Her reverie was interrupted by the sound of footsteps crunching through the forest just in front of her. Startled, she jumped up, dropping her pole. Her eyes were wide with fright. It was nearly dark now and Leanne was ready to take flight for the safety of her small house when the sound reached the clearing and a tall, dark-haired man dressed in jeans and a western shirt appeared.

"Sorry if I scared you, miss, but I believe that property across the creek is for sale?"

Her green eyes flashing, Leanne blurted angrily, "Yes, it is, but I would think that the proper thing to do would be to contact the owner before tramping through this property and scaring the neighbors to death!" Leanne knew she was out of line. After all, the man hadn't meant to scare her, and he had apologized. Trying to sound calmer, she extended a slender finger in the direction of her parents' home and said, "You'll find the owner in the brick house just up the hill there. His name is Rob Masterson."

Leanne bent to pick up her pole, only to find it had fallen into the water and drifted downstream. It had been one her father had given her as a child, and she couldn't bear to lose it. Looking at the handsome stranger and then at her runaway keepsake, Leanne ran her hands over her waist-length hair. Well, what did it matter to her what the man would think? She began to jog along the creek bank until she caught up with her pole; then she sloshed into the cold water to retrieve the old gift. As she looked up she was surprised to see the man smiling at her from across the narrow stream. She couldn't believe he had actually followed her. "I thought you wanted to buy some land," she charged.

"I did, but that can wait. Can I help you?" He took a step forward, extending a large hand in her direction. Ignoring his hand, Leanne helped herself out of the water, exiting on her own side of the creek. She looked down at her jeans and sneakers, now soaked, then back up into the devastating smile of the man.

"Must be a special pole," he said.

"It is," Leanne answered, feeling a bit foolish as she bent to squeeze water from the hem of her pants with one hand while clutching the pole with the other. In the corner of her eye, she could see the man as he folded his arms across his chest. A ridiculous grin on his face sent her temper soaring again. "It was a *gift!*" she explained, straightening.

"I see," he said, his voice betraying his amusement.

By now the evening shadows hid his features, but Leanne could still see the broad grin on his face. "May I ask what you find so funny?"

"Nothing," he quickly denied. "I was only thinking how lucky I am to have the original Ms. Huck Finn for a neighbor," he added with a chuckle.

Leanne's chin dropped. "You haven't bought the land yet," she retorted, starting back up the creek.

"Not yet," he echoed, following her from opposite the water. "But I will."

Ignoring him, Leanne turned toward her house, then glanced back over her shoulder. The man stood with his hands in his pockets, watching her. Leanne sighed heavily. She wasn't usually so rude to strangers. Why now? She wondered, turning to face him. "Is there anything else I can do for you?" she asked in an attempt to amend her bad manners.

"No thank you," he said with a smile. "I guess I'd better be on my way and let you get out of those wet clothes. I don't want to get off on a bad foot with my new neighbor." Before she could reply, the man had turned and was sauntering toward the brush, leaving her staring after him.

Several weeks had passed, but Leanne couldn't get the stranger out of her mind. It was spring, and Carlile's Department Store, where she worked as a purchasing agent, was receiving new merchandise. She was constantly busy and hadn't seen or heard from her parents, but she couldn't help wondering if the man had bought the land. She shouldn't have cared whether he had or not, but she was hoping that he hadn't.

Leanne locked her front door, shoving the keys into her jeans pocket as she descended the stairs of the redwood deck her father had built for her. Well, she would find out tonight as she was going to her parents' house for dinner. Walking up the shell road that led from her house to theirs, she wondered why her mother had sounded so strange when she called to invite her.

As she entered the dining room Leanne's green eyes

widened in surprise. The table was set with the best china, and her mother was placing a vase of fresh flowers on the table.

"Having company?" Leanne asked.

A look of guilt covered her mother's soft, round face as she replied, "Yes, dear. It was your father's idea not to tell you, but a Mr. Hall is coming to talk over some business and . . . well, you know your father. He wants you to meet someone nice, and according to him this Mr. Hall is the nicest kind of man. He hasn't told me much about him, of course; he was sure I would influence you, and he wants you to make your own judgments."

"As long as they are the same as his!" Leanne murmured as she made a face and sighed heavily. Then, seeing the anguish in her mother's eyes at having to excuse her father's matchmaking, she gave her a hug. "Who knows," she said, "maybe this will be my Prince Charming." Kissing her softly on the cheek, she added, "But, Mom, if it isn't, please try to convince Dad that I can find my own dates."

"I'm sure he knows that. You're a beautiful girl, and he just hates to see you brood so long over that engagement mess."

"Mother, it's been nearly six months and I assure you that I have gotten over Eric. It's just that I want some time to myself, time to pull my thoughts together as to what kind of man I want to marry, before I get myself back into a similar situation."

"Well, you know the old saying: 'You can't let one bad apple spoil the whole bushel'—or however that goes."

"Sharon, are you worrying about this girl again?"

"Hello, Dad," Leanne said, moving toward her father.

"Hi, princess," he replied, then continued talking to his wife. "Haven't I been telling you not to worry? This little Indian princess isn't going to be long without a young brave in her life." The handsome man with the reddish tan hugged his daughter. He had called her his Indian princess since her hair was first long enough to braid. Her tanned complexion, along with high cheekbones, gave the hint of an Indian ancestry. If not for her Irish green eyes, heavily fringed by long dark lashes, she could have been taken for a member of one of the local tribes.

"Set the silver, will you, Lea?" her mother asked, winking, as she turned to answer the doorbell, with her husband close behind her.

Leanne smiled to herself. They both knew who was doing the worrying. She loved her parents dearly and could well understand their concern. She was beginning to worry a little herself. Until she had seen the stranger at the creek, Leanne had wondered if she would ever thrill at the sight of a handsome man again. But he had stirred her senses back to life. She heard voices in the foyer, and as she placed the last knife on the table her father walked in with a man much taller than himself. She was so surprised that she barely heard her father say, "Leanne, meet Charles Bartholomew Hall. He's the new troubleshooter out at Delta, and after tonight he's going to be your new neighbor."

Leanne watched the man wince as her father introduced him using his full name. His rugged face softened, however, as he smiled. Leanne's heart started racing when the smile reached his hazel eyes.

"Please," he said in a deep voice. "Call me Bart." He had seemed familiar, but it wasn't until he spoke that Leanne was sure he was the man who had been at the creek. The same broad shoulders now strained against a cream silk shirt, and brown slacks rather than blue jeans covered his muscular thighs. His black hair was streaked with silver, and she guessed his age to be about thirty-five.

"And you are Leanne?" he asked as he took the hand she offered him and squeezed it gently.

"Oh . . . yes," she stuttered as she realized she had been staring. He hesitated before releasing her hand, and when he did, Leanne felt a twinge of disappointment. Her hand burned where he had touched it, and she rubbed it against her jeans to relieve the feeling. It was then that she realized how she was dressed. Her powder blue T-shirt with white letters reading Homeward Bound, together with her sneakers and ponytail, made her feel like a teenager. She wished she had at least worn a blouse with her jeans. She could change into one of her mother's, but that would be an obvious sign to her parents that she wanted to impress the man. And that was something she would avoid at all costs!

"How about those steaks, Sharon?" Leanne's father asked his wife.

"It shouldn't be long now. Will you check them for me, Rob, while I pour the iced tea?"

"Sure. Come on, Bart. Watch the chef at work."

Bart followed Robert Masterson through a sliding glass door that led to the patio. When they had shut the door, Leanne's mother breathed a sigh of relief. "That father of yours!"

"Yes, but he's your husband!" Leanne laughed and began to fill the salad bowls on a nearby cart while her mother filled crystal glasses with ice. "I wish you had told me you were having such a nice dinner, Mom. I would have dressed a little better."

"Oh, Lea, you look fine, but it isn't my dinner you're worried about dressing up for. I saw the sparkle in your eyes when *he* walked in the door."

"Mother, that's nonsense! I simply feel uncomfortable wearing jeans while I eat from china." Leanne knew she shouldn't have said anything. Her parents were always jumping to conclusions. As her mother went to the kitchen for the tea Leanne finished filling the salad bowls. The trouble was, this time her mother was right; she *was* taken with the strange man, much to her chagrin. After placing a bowl of salad at each setting, Leanne took the serving bowl into the kitchen to wash and passed her mother carrying out the tea. As she rinsed the bowl her thoughts raced. Did he recognize her? Why should he? It had been nearly dark, and if it weren't for his deep, husky voice, she wouldn't have been sure about him.

"How long are you going to rinse that bowl?"

Leanne nearly dropped the clear glass container as she whirled around to see her mother at the doorway.

Sharon Masterson laughed sweetly and said, "You can't fool me, Leanne Marie! That young man has you shaken."

Leanne let out an exaggerated breath, picked up the crock of baked potatoes and pranced out of the kitchen, saying, "You're as bad as Dad!"

"And what's wrong with me?" she heard her father

ask lightheartedly as she came through the swinging door from the kitchen into the dining room, the aroma of hickory smoke wafting through the air.

Leanne laughed a little shakily and said, "Not a thing, Dad." Tongs in hand, she placed a steaming baked potato on each of the cherry-blossom plates, thanking God for not having to explain to her father what she had meant. She was aware of a tickling sensation on the back of her neck as she passed in front of Bart, who was watching her while her father rattled on and on about Delta's new oil site.

Mrs. Masterson came in with a silver lazy Susan decorated with crystal dishes containing colorful relishes placed between butter, sour cream and salad dressings. The table was set beautifully, with two chairs on either side and candlesticks on each end. A vase of flowers stood next to each candle. Leanne could never remember having felt so uncomfortable at her mother's table as she realized that the seating arrangements meant she would sit next to Bart, with her parents across from them. Bart held her chair for her, and she sat down as gracefully as she could, though her attire made her feel like a clumsy tomboy.

Rob Masterson said a brief prayer over their dinner, and as they ate, Leanne listened to her parents question Bart about his travels as an oil consultant, inserting only enough conversation on her part to be polite.

"Why on earth would you give up such an exciting job?" Mrs. Masterson asked, her eyes bright with interest.

"I still travel, Mrs. Masterson, but only in the States now," Bart answered before he bit into the savory steak.

"Yes, but to travel abroad . . ." Leanne's mother was in awe of Bart's travels and didn't understand his giving up the glamorous occupation. Shaking her head slowly, she said, "I don't think I would have made your choice, Mr. Hall."

"Well, you see, it took me away from home three weeks out of the month, and I decided my children need to have a chance to get to know their father before they think they haven't got one." Bart smiled, piercing another slice of steak with his fork.

Leanne choked on the tea she had just sipped and hoped her surprise hadn't been obvious. Served her dad right, she thought, disappointed to hear the man was attached to some other "lucky" woman.

Sharon Masterson was surprised as well, and she didn't bother to hide it. "But Rob said you weren't married."

God, please, no, Leanne prayed silently. She wanted to cry from embarrassment, but that would only make matters worse. Maybe Mr. Hall couldn't read between the lines. Maybe he wouldn't catch on that her parents had hopes for him and their old-maid daughter. Leanne continued to cut her steak slowly, using as much control as possible. God, *please* get me through this night. She swallowed hard and bravely carried the conversation in the most natural direction she could think of. "How many children do you have, Mr. Hall?"

Bart turned his dark head in her direction for the first time all evening, his hazel eyes smiling. Leanne endured his gaze for as long as she could, then lowered her lashes to study the dark hairs on the back of his tanned hand resting near hers. "I have two boys, *Miss* Masterson. Mathew is seven and Charlie is nine."

Leanne winced at the emphasis he had put on *Miss*. She knew he was referring to the way she had spoken to him in a formal manner. What was it to him? she thought; he's a married man. Leanne stole a glance at her father, who sat silently eating with a devilish smile on his face.

Bart turned his gaze to Leanne's mother and, reaching for his tea glass, held it in midair as he said, "Rob was right, Mrs. Masterson." He took a drink of tea, replacing the glass on the table and looking at Leanne as he added, "My wife died a little over two years ago."

"Oh, I'm sorry," the older woman said, embarrassed.

"No need to be sorry, really," he said reassuringly, a warm smile curving his full lips. "As I said, it's been two years now. It wasn't long after Carol's death that I started traveling, and the boys have been staying with their grandmother ever since. I've decided to settle down and try to make up for the time I've wasted."

"Won't your traveling in the States take you away from home, too?" Leanne asked, curious about this stranger who was slowly ingratiating himself into her heart with his sincere love for his children.

"To an extent, but there will be many times when the boys can go with me. I'll be bringing them out to see the property next weekend. Maybe you could teach us how to fish?" His smiling gaze captured Leanne's. He had recognized her, after all. She was so surprised she couldn't speak the words forming in her mouth.

"She'd love to." Rob Masterson's booming voice filled the air after keeping silent throughout the conversation.

"But, Dad . . ."

"How about more coffee and dessert in the living

room, honey?" he said to his wife as he stood, ignoring Leanne's protest. "It's time Bart and I talked a little money. Come on, Bart," he called over his shoulder as he left the room.

"Be right with you, Rob. Thank you for dinner, Mrs. Masterson," Bart said as he rose from his chair. "You didn't have to go to so much trouble, but your table was beautiful and the food delicious. Not to mention the charming company." He smiled down at Leanne. "By the way, you never said. Will you be busy on Saturday?"

Leanne felt at a disadvantage as he stood towering over her, his large hand on the back of her chair, his devastating eyes piercing hers. Why did he affect her this way? She'd better beware, or she would end up hurt again. "I'm sorry, Mr. Hall, but I'm afraid I already have plans. I've promised to help Mother turn her garden and get it ready for—"

"Leanne, now, you know your father and I can do that by ourselves," her mother interrupted as she began to stack the dishes.

"Yes, Mom, I know, but I've planned on it and I'd really like to help." She watched Bart's dark brows raise as he shrugged his heavy shoulders.

"Sunday, then?"

"Leanne teaches Sunday school on Sundays," Mrs. Masterson put in before she left the room carrying a pile of plates.

Thank you, Mother, Leanne thought with a sigh of relief.

"All right. Another time, then."

"Yes, another time."

"Leanne, let the man come pay me for that place,

and then you can have him all to yourself." Leanne felt the blood rush to her face as her father's good-natured joking embarrassed her again.

After they had cleared the table, Leanne and her mother took a tray of fresh coffee and tea cakes into the living room. Her father carried the conversation through dessert, and finally Leanne felt it was safe to say good night.

"Nonsense, girl. You have nothing but that empty house to go back to. Stay a while," her father said as she stood to go.

"No, really, Dad. I've had a long day and I have some things to do around the house yet."

"Well, okay, princess."

Leanne bent over and placed a kiss on his rough cheek. "Good night, Dad." Squeezing her mother's hand, she added, "'Night, Mom. Dinner was wonderful."

Bart had stood and was waiting in the arched doorway that led to the foyer. "May I take you home, Miss Masterson?"

"Leanne. Her name's Leanne." Her father was doing it again. "And that's a good idea, Bart. She walks over here, and it's pretty dark out."

"No, really, I'd rather walk," Leanne stated firmly. "I enjoy it."

"So do I," Bart said, his hazel eyes shining. "I'll walk with you." He took her elbow and led her to the front door, with Mr. and Mrs. Masterson following them. "I'll say good night, too," Bart said as they went outside. "After I see . . . Leanne home, I'll be leaving.

It was nice meeting you, Mrs. Masterson, and thank you again for dinner. I'll see you tomorrow, Rob." He propelled her down the walkway, Leanne calling good night once more before her parents closed the door and left her alone in the moonlight with Bart.

They walked silently along the road, Bart's hand at her waist and her heart in her throat. The silence was broken only by the soft, crunching noise of their feet on the shells and the occasional croaking of a bullfrog. Unable to stand the quiet any longer, Leanne spoke. "This really isn't necessary, you know. I walk this road all the time, and it's perfectly safe."

"I'm sure it is."

"But you'll have to walk all the way back for your car."

"Then you should have let me drive you."

"You didn't have to do either!" Leanne said, speeding up her pace so that she walked a few steps ahead of him, forcing his hand to drop from her waist.

Bart's long strides soon brought him even with her again. "Do you dislike me, or are you always this rude?"

"I'm not being rude. I just don't need to be watched over. I can take care of myself."

"Is that why you live a half mile from your parents? Are you so afraid of being alone with a man that you'd rather walk than accept a courteous gesture?"

"That's not fair!" Leanne swung around to face him, anger flashing in her green eyes. "What do you know about me? Nothing! And that's all you're going to know!" Leanne turned on her heel and stomped down the road, hearing his footsteps behind her. When she reached the house, she scrambled up the stairs of the redwood deck and pulled a set of keys from her jeans pocket. The nerve of that man! She burned all over with fury. How dare he speak to her that way? She fumbled with the key nervously, then turned quickly as she felt the deck give with added weight.

"Let me help you," Bart said. He flipped his cigarette lighter and lit the area around the doorknob, enabling her to see the lock.

"Thank you," she bit out, more angry with herself for not leaving on the porch light than with him. The latch clicked and so did the lighter. She replaced her key in her jeans and moved to turn the knob, only to feel the exciting warmth of Bart's hand under hers. Quickly she pulled her hand back and allowed him to open the door.

"Still afraid of me?"

"I'm not afraid of you!" she said defensively. But she was afraid—of what, she didn't know for sure.

"Then go out with me Friday night," he said as he leaned with one hand resting against the wall above her head.

"I might have to work."

"You and I both know that's an excuse."

"All right, all right! If I don't have to work, I'll go." She had to leave herself some kind of out. The man did things to her senses that she couldn't control, and she didn't like it.

His hazel eyes searched her face thoughtfully. "What are you afraid of?" he insisted.

"Nothing." Leanne moved to go inside, but suddenly his hands were on her arms, pulling her close to him.

The smell of his musk after-shave filled her head, and his soft breath whispered against her lips.

"Are you afraid of this?" She felt his full lips press warmly against hers, draining her of reality. But the kiss ended as suddenly as it had begun, and when he released her she was stunned until his quiet words broke the spell. "That wasn't so bad, now, was it?" Furious, she slapped him and ran into the house, slamming the door in his face.

Leanne spent the next few days groping for answers to Bart's question. What *was* she afraid of? Of being hurt again, or of giving in to her desires? *Had* she moved close to her parents for a sense of security? Why did this man have to come into her life? She left her desk and went down the hall toward Stephen's office. Her relationship with him was so uncomplicated; his kisses were so warm and sincere. He would never be as demanding as Bart had been. But Stephen didn't excite her the way Bart did, either.

Besides the problems in her personal life, Leanne was having difficulties at work. Several people were out sick, leaving departments shorthanded, including Stephen's office. He had flown to Dallas and asked that she fill the vacancies. She had managed to fill all of the major ones but had not been prepared when the evening personnel for sporting goods called to say they wouldn't be in. Fumbling through Stephen's file, she found several names to call, but none of the people were able to work. Exasperated, Leanne checked the time: four-thirty. She had half an hour to grab something to eat before the first shift got off; then she would simply fill in herself. Her black silk shirt and gray slacks were rumpled, but at least they would be comfortable.

She was waiting on a couple buying bowling balls for their first summer league when she felt a familiar fluttering in her stomach. Glancing over her shoulder, she saw Bart leaning against the sales counter, his arms folded across his chest and a mischievous smile in his hazel eyes. What was he doing here? she wondered.

"Can we have the holes drilled here?" the man asked after he and his wife had decided on which balls they wanted.

"Yes," she answered, trying to calm her racing heart. "I'll measure your grip now, but the man who bores the holes won't be in until Monday."

"That will be fine. The league doesn't start for another month. We just want time to get used to the new balls."

Leanne took the couple over to the counter to measure their grips and did her best to ignore the man standing purposely in her way. She had had a long week and hadn't expected to spend the last day of it working twelve hours. Her patience was short and she was in no mood to be harassed, but though she tried to ignore him, Bart's mere presence was distracting. "Can I help you, sir?" she finally asked sarcastically.

"Yes, but I can wait until you're finished here."

"Thank you," she said between gritted teeth, her green eyes narrowing and her fingers moving decisively against the register keys as she rang up the total. She gave the couple their receipt, and after they had walked away, she turned to Bart. "What are you doing here?" she asked, placing her hands on her slim hips. Not waiting for his answer, she added, "And how did you

know where to find me? I never said where I worked."
Even as she asked the question, she knew the answer.

"Your father was very accommodating."

Just as she thought. Well, she was just going to have
to have a little talk with dear Dad!

"Actually, I came to apologize for the other night."

"Well, you should." Leanne watched a dark brow
arch and felt a little ashamed for being so rude.
"Apology accepted," she said in an attempt to be more
friendly.

"Now, that's what I like. A forgiving soul." He
leaned forward, his arms resting against the counter-
top.

Anger welled up inside her. "Well, don't push your
luck," she retorted, and began to straighten the display
of literature next to his arm.

His smiling eyes were irresistible, and to avoid them
Leanne stooped to rearrange the shelves under the
counter. The best thing to do was to ignore him, she
thought. But he was still standing there when she had
finished.

"Was there something else you wanted to say?"

"We had a date, remember?"

"I'm working," she stated matter-of-factly.

"I can see that. When do you get off?"

"It doesn't matter. I'll be tired," she said, her fingers
playing with the metal of her silver belt buckle.

"Then I'll just hang around here for a while." Bart
straightened, the mauve shirt straining against the
muscles of his back, his hands set loosely in the pockets
of his tan slacks.

"That's loitering, and it's not allowed," Leanne said,
shocked that he would be so persistent. "I could get in

trouble if someone noticed." She moved from behind the counter and began sorting fishing lures that had been misplaced by browsing customers.

Bart followed her, saying, "Not if I'm buying something." He ran a hand up the length of a fishing rod, inspecting the details. "What about a reel for this rod?" Bart pulled the long, green rod with its cork-covered handle off the rack, moving back to the counter where the reels were housed.

Leanne had no choice but to wait on him, and she did so in a businesslike manner. He took his time, wanting to see every reel in the case and even asking about a few she didn't have. She looked the model numbers up in the reference book and made a note to order them. She felt him watching her as she flipped through the pages and knew without looking up that his eyes were smiling.

"How long have you been working at Carlile's?"

"Since I was in high school," she said nonchalantly, ringing up his purchases and praying she wouldn't make a mistake. His nearness made her nervous.

"Why haven't I seen you?"

"For the past two years I've been working in the purchasing department."

"And tonight?" he asked, playing with a pencil on the counter.

"We were shorthanded and Stephen . . . Mr. Carlile is out of town, so I'm filling in."

"You're doing a very good job. Do you have to fill in for Carlile often?"

"Only when it's necessary," she said as she finished bagging his merchandise.

"Where did you learn so much about fishing?" Bart

took the bag from her and set it on the floor next to him.

"My father wanted a son but got me instead!" Leanne found herself laughing and wondered when it was that she had begun to find it so easy to talk to him.

"Looks to me as though he got a better deal. A beautiful daughter who knows about fishing, too. Your father must be a good teacher."

"I started in sporting goods when I was seventeen," she confessed. "But Dad is a good teacher," she added, feeling as if she had just been disloyal to her father's teaching ability.

Bart gave her an admiring smile and was about to speak when he was interrupted by a loud crash. They both turned in time to see two young boys dash down an aisle and out of sight. Leanne hurried to see what had fallen and found a pile of fishing rods tangled together on the floor. As she began to rehang them on the rack Bart came from behind her, holding two reluctant boys by the arm.

"What shall we do with them? Hang them by their toes till they tell us their names?" Bart's eyes danced with mischief.

"My name's Marvin Dayne," the older boy volunteered. "And that's my brother, Billy."

Bart and Leanne laughed, and hesitantly the puzzled boys joined them.

"Do you think you could hang these poles back?" Leanne asked.

"Yes, ma'am!" the boys chimed in unison.

Bart let them go and they began to clean the mess they had made. Leanne supervised and Bart helped.

"Did you boys want to buy a rod?" she asked.

"Well, tomorrow's Dad's birthday and we—"

"I see," Leanne interrupted. "How much money do you have?"

"Only fifteen dollars." The older boy made a face and pulled several dollar bills and some change out of his pocket.

"Not enough, is it?" the younger boy asked.

"I think we could work something out." She pulled a rod off the rack and walked over to the counter. Bart stood with his parcels in hand and a smile on his handsome face.

"Looks like you've got things under control, so I'll be leaving."

"Thank you for your help. These boys would have never come back for their gift if you hadn't caught them." The boys giggled and poked each other with their elbows.

"You boys behave yourselves, now. I'll see you tomorrow," he said to Leanne as he winked and walked away.

Chapter Two

Leanne awoke with a groan as she reached for the receiver. A persistent ringing was followed by a hard knock, and she realized that there was someone at the door, not on the phone. She replaced the receiver and hurriedly grabbed her robe. A glance at the digital clock next to the phone told her it was five-thirty. Something must be wrong with Mom or Dad, she thought. She was shuffling along the narrow hallway when the knock sounded again. "I'm coming," she called, tripping over the edge of the carpet. When she reached the door, she groped for the porch light switch but flooded the living room with light instead. She blinked her sleepy eyes and reached for the latch, stopping as she realized it might not be either of her parents.

"Who is it?" she called through the door.

A deep masculine voice answered, "It's Bart."

Suddenly she was wide awake. She swung the door open, and the light fell across Bart's contagious smile. "What are you doing here? Is something wrong?" Surely he would not be smiling if something was wrong!

"Nothing's wrong, but we have some fish to catch, and if we don't hurry there will be some hungry people come breakfast."

Leanne was furious. How dare he wake her at this hour after she had said she wouldn't go! "Bart Hall, I told you—"

"But I told the boys that you were an expert fisherwoman!" Leanne heard the muffled sound again, only this time she recognized it as stifled giggles. Her eyes traveled to Bart's waist as she leaned forward to see past him. Bart moved aside, and the light revealed two small figures in the shadows. Leanne sighed, running her fingers through her mussed hair. She was a pushover for children, and Bart must have figured that out at the store last night. It was a mean trick and she'd have to figure a way to get even, but for now, it seemed, she was going fishing.

"Well, come out of the shadows and let me see who I'll be fishing with today," she said, flipping on the porch light.

"He's Mathew and I'm Charlie," the older boy said bravely as he tugged on his brother's arm.

Charlie was a miniature replica of his father, even down to his arrogant tone of voice. Such a young thing to sound so old. Mathew was shy and still had the honey-blonde hair that his older brother was losing to a darker brown. Freckles dotted each of their little noses, although Mathew had twice as many as Charlie.

"Hello," Leanne said, smiling down at them.

"Mathew, Charlie, meet Miss Masterson," Bart introduced them courteously.

"Are you really an . . . expert . . . fisherwoman?" Mathew asked shyly from behind Bart's jeans-clad legs. They all laughed, Leanne surrendering her anger in exchange for the fun the day seemed to promise.

"I don't know about that, Mathew, but I do like to fish, and judging from your faces, I guess I'd better get ready. Should I make coffee and hot chocolate?"

"Dad brought everything," Charlie's grown-up voice told her.

"Okay, I'll be right out, then," she said as she shut the door, leaving them sitting on the deck chairs waiting for her.

Quickly she changed into jeans and a short-sleeved burgundy pullover, then moved to the bathroom to wash up. "What a mess!" she gasped when she saw her reflection in the mirror. Her hair lay in confused ringlets about her shoulders, her face was free of makeup, and her eyes were still puffy and red. A small knock on the front door warned her to hurry, and as she called "Come in" she ran a brush quickly through her hair. That was a mistake. The bristles tangled in the fine strands and she couldn't see to untangle them. She pulled at her hair, frustrated with herself for being so foolish.

"Ahem." A small voice caught her attention. Looking up, she saw Mathew standing at the open door. "Could I . . . ?"

"Oh, yes, Mathew, come on in." She stepped out of the bathroom and allowed him to enter and shut the door. Moving to a mirror in the living room, Leanne again tried to untangle the brush.

"Need some help?" Bart asked, startling her, as she hadn't heard him come in. She glanced at the open front door, with Charlie still on the deck. "Matt left the door open," Bart explained. "Looks like you're in trouble here."

"I can't seem to untangle the brush," Leanne said, irritated that he should catch her in such a predicament. Struggling to free the brush, Leanne was surprised when she felt Bart's warm hands cover hers and move them aside.

"Let me," he said. She closed her eyes, expecting pain when he tugged at the hair, but he didn't tug and there was no pain, only a chill that ran up her spine. "Cold? You'd better wear a sweater; it's still crisp out." Little did he know it was the excitement of his touch that caused her to shiver.

Bart freed the brush and ran it gently over the dark silk of her hair. It was an intimate gesture that Leanne wasn't prepared for, and, moving away from him, she said, "Thank you." Bart smiled and handed her the brush, watching as she pulled her hair away from her face to fasten it at the back of her neck.

Mathew came scampering down the hall excitedly. "Hey, Charlie, she's got a fish tank in the bathroom! With a shark in it, too!"

"In the bathroom?" Charlie had to see, too, and Leanne laughed as she explained to Bart that it was a tropical fish.

As they finally stepped out the door Leanne could see where Bart had built a fire on the rocks near the water. He was right; the air was crisp even though it was already April.

Hours passed and Leanne laid her pole next to her, drawing her legs up, hugging them to her as she watched the sun peep over the hills. She loved the pink clouds against the soft blue of the sky. Resting her chin on her knees, she watched Bart help Mathew bring a flopping catfish in and take it off the hook. His children had already captured her heart; how long would it be before he did the same? Bart looked up as Mathew ran along the bank carrying his fish. His eyes held hers for a moment; then she slowly turned to Mathew as he reached her and said breathlessly, "Dad said if you were ready, we could have breakfast now." Leanne smiled at the freckle-faced boy and knew he must be starving.

"Sure, Mathew. Let's get everything ready." She stirred the fire and placed a grill across it. She was getting a cast-iron skillet out of a box Bart had brought when he and Charlie walked up.

"Charlie and I will cook if you and Mathew will clean the fish," Bart said teasingly as he held a long string of fish in her direction.

Leanne stood with one hand on her hip and the pan in the other hand. "I hate to tell you, but I make a better fisherwoman than I do a fish cleaner."

The boys laughed heartily and Bart said, "Since she has a weapon, Charlie, I guess we'd better get these fish cleaned." Leanne looked from Bart to the heavy skillet and laughed as she realized what he meant.

Mathew helped Leanne set a rock slab with a table-cloth and paper plates that they found in the box. "This is fun," he said happily. "We didn't ever have fish for breakfast before. What else are we gonna have?" he asked, digging into the box curiously.

"Well, let's see," Leanne said, opening the ice chest and finding soft drinks, a carton of eggs, and frozen hashbrowns that were not so frozen anymore. There was also a package of wieners, as well as mustard and relish.

"That's for supper," Mathew said. Leanne took the hashbrowns and eggs out and added oil to the skillet. Bart and Charlie rinsed the fish in the creek, and after she had mealed them, Leanne dropped them into the hot oil, saving the hashbrowns and eggs until the fish were finished.

"Fish doesn't go good for breakfast," Mathew said as he finished his eggs and potatoes, leaving a large portion of fish on his plate.

"Tastes good to me," Charlie said, reaching for more.

"Taste good to you, Miss Leanne?" Mathew asked.

"It takes some getting used to, I admit, but it is good to me." Mathew made a face and took another bite of fish.

"It's okay, Matt, you don't have to eat it," Bart said, reaching for the plate. He put the other plates under it and dropped them into a plastic bag. Leanne helped him clean up and put out the fire while the boys tossed stones in the water before settling down on the creek bank.

"Thank you for coming," Bart said sincerely as he folded the tablecloth. "The boys have really enjoyed having you along."

"They are darlings," she replied, wiping the skillet clean.

"I don't know if *darlings* is the right word; little devils would be more like it," he said, smiling as he looked past her. Leanne followed his gaze. Charlie sat leaning against a tree with Mathew's head in his lap, both asleep. She was touched at the unashamed love their father had for them.

"Would you like to take them inside?" Leanne asked, motioning to her house.

"I have sleeping bags in the truck," he said, still gazing at the children, his hands thrust into his pockets. Turning to Leanne, he added, "We're camping out here tonight."

She followed him to the black truck parked next to her small foreign car. They settled the boys on sleeping bags, and as they walked back to the cooking site Leanne said, "I've really enjoyed it, but I do need to help my parents this morning."

Bart gently took her arm, turning her to face him. "You don't want to leave me by myself, now, do you?"

Her heart racing, Leanne fought to control her voice. "I'm sure you can entertain yourself." She felt his hand slide up her arm, and an involuntary shiver betrayed her. His eyes smiled a knowing smile and as he pulled her into his arms she realized how easy it would be to fall in love with him. His mouth came down to capture hers and as the kiss deepened, Leanne couldn't control her response. Her arms moved under his, clinging to his broad back. Her legs grew weak, his hold tightening as she leaned against him for support.

The familiar sound of stifled giggles brought Leanne

back to reality with a jolt. Her face grew warm and she pulled away from Bart's intoxicating touch, turning to glance quickly at Mathew and Charlie, whose faces were beaming. Trying to regain her breath, she said quietly, "I've got to be going now."

Bart searched her face. "We'll be seeing you later, then," he said, his voice low.

Leanne walked slowly up the gravel road, staring absently at the broken shells under her feet. Was she crazy, falling into his arms like that? Hadn't she learned her lesson with Eric? But Bart was so different, she argued with herself, her fingertips touching her lips. Yes, and so much more dangerous, she thought. With Eric, she had at least *thought* that she was in control.

Sharon Masterson answered the door, the look on her face changing from expectant to disappointed. Looking past Leanne, she asked, "Where's Bart and the children?"

"Back at the creek. Why?" Leanne asked, following her mother into the kitchen.

"Well, he said that after you guys fished you would all be coming over to help with the garden, and I said I'd fix lunch. I thought I'd make . . ." Leanne wasn't listening. She was angry with Bart. He had been so sure she would go fishing!

"Oooh!" she exclaimed, frustrated that he had gotten his way.

"What is it, Leanne? Should I make something else?" Her mother asked, surprised at her daughter's reaction to chicken salad.

"What else?" she asked absently, sinking into a chair.

"My goodness. Aren't we in a good mood today."

"I'm sorry, Mom. What were you saying?"

"Never mind. Just get yourself a cup of coffee and join us on the patio, but pull yourself together, will you?"

The telephone rang and Leanne poured herself a cup of coffee, leaving her mother to answer it as she joined her father outside.

"Morning, princess," he said from behind the small tractor he was working on.

"Hi, Dad," she answered, expelling an exaggerated breath.

"What is it?" he asked, moving to the patio table to join her.

"Your friend, Bartholomew, is just a little too chauvinistic for me."

"Oh?" Rob Masterson grinned before sipping his coffee.

The patio door slid open and Mrs. Masterson carried a coffee pot and hot pad to the table.

"That was Ken on the phone," she said, a worried frown on her brow.

"What's the great man got you upset about this time?" her husband asked her as he slammed his cup on the table.

"He's my brother, Rob, and I'm glad he feels he can talk to me."

"Sure, but it'd be nice if he'd listen to you too!"

"It's Rhonda again, isn't it, Mother?" Leanne asked, concerned for her cousin.

"Yes." Mrs. Masterson refilled their cups and then added, "He's so worried about her being in California, but he won't admit it."

"No, but he sure calls you every time he hears about a quake or a mugging."

Leanne knew her father was concerned for his wife. He got irritated every time she was upset, but only because he didn't know what to do about it. She watched as he took her mother's hand.

"I'm sorry, Sherry," he said. "The good Lord knows Ken needs our prayers as much as our advice." He sighed heavily and stood. "Guess I could use a few prayers too!"

We all could, Leanne thought as she heard Bart and the boys approaching. She had been impatient to tell him how furious she was, but when he rounded the corner with a boyish grin on his face, she felt the anger fade away.

They spent the afternoon with her parents, and at the approach of evening Leanne joined Bart and the boys when they returned to camp. As they neared the creek Leanne saw where Bart had built a crude bridge out of logs, and as she looked past the trees on Bart's property she could make out a tent.

When they reached the bridge, the boys scampered across, delighted with the adventure. Leanne hesitated looking first at Bart, then at the bridge. "Is it safe?" she asked teasingly, but his answer was more than she asked for as he scooped her up into his arms and stepped onto the bridge. "Bart!" she screamed, and thrashed about, trying to get down.

"Be still, now, or I'll drop you." Leanne looked down at the cold water. It was only a foot or so below the bridge, but she didn't want to fall in. Reluctantly, she clung to his strong shoulders. He smelled of smoke mingled with musk after-shave. Leanne could almost taste the sweetness of his kiss, though he never gave it. The feel of his powerful arms around her was comforting, and she didn't want the feeling to end when they reached the other side.

He stood her next to him, keeping his arm across her back as they walked through the woods, calling Mathew and Charlie, who were chasing a squirrel. Bart showed her the spot where he wanted to build a cabin. It was halfway between the creek and the highway that ran in front of his property.

"Will it be a weekend place, or do you plan to live in it?" Leanne asked as she found an old stump to sit on.

Bart stood next to her, his hands in his pockets. "I would like to move out here," he said, leaning back to look at the sky through the treetops. Then, placing his foot on the fallen log next to her, he leaned forward, resting his arms across his leg before adding, "Especially since I've come to enjoy my neighbor's company so much." He pulled at a loose strand of her hair and straightened. "But it would be hard to get a housekeeper to come out here." His eyes roamed her figure. "That is, unless you would be willing to keep house for me?" His hazel eyes smiled daringly into hers.

Leanne blushed. "Then what would Carlile's do when they were shorthanded?"

"That's right. Carlile would be lost without you."

Leanne thought she detected a note of cynicism in his voice. "Do you know Stephen?"

"You might say that. He was dating my kid sister when his grandfather died, leaving him his fortune. She was good enough for him *until then*." Bart stared into the forest, a hard look covering his features.

"Have you seen Stephen lately?"

"Not in two years. I haven't had any reason to. Why?"

"Because he's changed a lot in the last year or so."

"What did he do? Run out of money?" he asked sarcastically.

"No, but he's experienced something special, and it's changed his attitude toward people and life in general. He isn't as hung up on money as he used to be. In fact, he now donates a good portion of his inheritance to various charities."

"That's a good write-off."

"What do you mean?"

"Taxes. Charities make good tax write-offs."

"Bart, give the man a break! How can you judge him when you haven't seen him in two years?"

"Linda cried for months after he dropped her. Carlile's life might have changed for the better, but Linda hasn't been the same ever since she met him."

He really hates Stephen, she thought. Eric had hurt her, but she had been able to forgive him . . . as long as she never had to see him again. A smile tugged at the corners of her mouth.

"What's the secret?"

"No secret. I just . . ." Should she tell him about Eric? If she didn't explain, he might misinterpret her thoughts. "It's just that I . . . I know how your sister must have felt."

"I see. And how would you know that?" Bart said as he sat on the log, eyeing her curiously.

"I was once in a similar situation. I was engaged to a man I'd known for two years when I found out he was engaged to someone else." Leanne picked at a loose thread in the hem of her shirt.

"Ah. That explains your attitude toward men. I was beginning to wonder if I had two heads or something."

Leanne laughed halfheartedly. "I was thinking how I didn't hold a grudge against him, but I guess I do."

"As long as I don't have to pay for his mistake," Bart said, looking into her green eyes. Leanne quickly averted her gaze to watch the boys building a fort out of fallen limbs and brush.

They watched the boys play until dark; then all moved back to the tent site, where they roasted hot dogs and marshmallows. "Have you ever had smores?" Leanne asked when they had eaten.

"Smores?" Mathew repeated with a frown on his small face.

"They're good. In fact, that's why they're called smores. They're so good you keep asking for 'some more.'" Mathew's frown deepened as he didn't understand the joke.

"Some more. Get it?" Charlie asked Mathew, laughing.

"Oh," Mathew said, laughing too. "I get it. Smore."

Charlie walked with Leanne to her house and they brought back graham crackers and chocolate bars. She took their roasted marshmallows and placed them along with a chocolate bar between two crackers. She watched the boys' faces light up as they devoured the scrumptious treat.

"Hey, Dad, she knows a lot of neat stuff," Charlie said as he took another bite.

"Yeah. An expert fisherwoman and an expert cook, too," Mathew said, his grin trimmed with chocolate.

"Thank you, boys," she said, standing and brushing

off her pants. "I've had a marvelous day, but I've got to get going."

"But it's still early," Bart said, rising to join her.

"I know, but I teach Sunday school and need to go over my plans a little. Besides, this is a time for you to spend with your children—alone," she said, emphasizing the last word before Bart could insist.

Mathew ran up to her and hugged her. "Can we see you next time?"

She lifted the small, thin boy into her arms. "Of course, Mathew." An idea came to her, and she looked from Mathew to Bart, smiling impishly. "Matter of fact, your dad is going to help me supervise a roller-skating party for a bunch of kids just about your age, and you and Charlie are invited." Leanne nearly burst as she held back the laughter that bubbled inside her. That would be a perfect way to get even with Bart for trapping her into fishing, though now she was glad that he had.

"Just how many children?" Bart asked, folding his arms across his chest, squinting his eyes in mock anger.

"About twelve; fourteen counting Mathew and Charlie."

"Where did you come up with twelve . . . ?"

"My Sunday school class. We've had it planned for weeks, and I was at a loss as to who would help me." She sat Mathew down and kissed his cheek. "Good night, honey," she said, then moved toward Charlie. He hesitated before raising his cheek to accept her kiss. "Good night, Charlie. See you next Friday," Leanne called over her shoulder as she made her way toward the creek.

"Wait," Bart said, his long strides catching up with

her. "It's dark out. Let me walk you." He glanced at Mathew and Charlie. "You boys stay right there till I get back. And don't get too close to the fire, either."

"This isn't necessary," Leanne protested. "It's just a few yards, remember?" She felt his arm around her and knew he was vexed with her for not needing him.

They walked in silence until they reached the bridge, and Leanne didn't object when he lifted her in his arms and carried her across.

"Good night," she said as she slid to the ground.

"No good-night kiss for me?" he asked in a husky tone, his face close to hers.

Leanne sighed. The man was impossible; didn't he realize how hard she was fighting the emotions he stirred? She stood on tiptoe and placed a kiss on his now-prickly cheek. Perhaps he did know how hard she was fighting, and maybe he also knew, as she did, that it was a losing battle.

"Good night," she said again as she turned toward home.

Chapter Three

"Aren't you going to skate?" Bart asked Leanne above the music as they stood at the railing watching children pass them. Some were on their fifth time around, while others were still making their first.

"Not me! I came to watch!" Charlie whizzed by them, turning to wave as he coasted backward. "Can you skate?" she asked Bart.

"Not well," he said, making a face as he leaned forward, resting his elbows on the railing with his arms extended in front of him.

Leanne tried to imagine this self-possessed man out on the floor, arms thrashing as he kept his balance. "I'll skate if you will," she said daringly. "Maybe I could even help you." She'd better be careful, she thought. She didn't skate too well herself, but it would be worth a few bruises to see Bart sprawled in the middle of the floor.

He accepted her challenge, and Leanne helped him with his roller skates. They scooted across the carpet toward the rink, Bart gripping her waist so hard she thought he would make her fall. When their skates touched the smooth surface, Bart swayed, nearly tumbling, but caught his balance just in time. Frowning, Leanne began to regret her idea. How humiliated he would be, she thought.

"Bart, are you sure you want to try this?" she asked, a look of concern on her face as he ventured away from her.

"Sure I'm sure," he said, flashing Leanne a quick smile, losing his balance again. He reached for her and she quickly went to his aid.

Soon they were making their way around the large circle, Leanne proud of Bart's efforts and ashamed of herself. A string of children zoomed past them, causing Leanne to stumble, her skates slipping. Her last thought was a vision of Bart collapsing on top of her. But he didn't fall; instead, he held her up. He had had his finger hooked in the belt loop of her jeans, and Leanne wished he had let her drop, as she felt ridiculous bent over with her feet and arms dangling in the air. She was finally able to straighten by clinging to Bart's free arm. She stood facing him; his hands were at her waist, hers were resting on his arms. She was amazed that he had been able to keep from falling. Suddenly the lights dimmed and a voice came over the public-address system announcing that the next song was for couples only. Leanne's eyes widened as Bart skated backward, pulling her with him, her face growing red with rage while he smiled down at her. Lashing out at him, she lost control of her skates again and was forced to lean against his hard frame until she regained it.

"You tricked me!" she blurted when she had her balance back.

"Wasn't that what you were going to do to me?"

Leanne glanced down. "Well, yes, but I really felt terrible about it, and you don't feel terrible at all."

Bart pulled her close to him again and chuckled. "Yes, I do. I feel terrible every time I'm away from you. So when are you going to go out with me?"

"I am 'out' with you," Leanne answered, moving her feet methodically to the music, following his perfect lead. If he affected her so strongly in public, what would it be like to be alone with him? She wasn't sure she wanted to find out.

"How about it?"

"How about what?" He was driving her mad, and she wished he would let her go before she unashamedly threw herself into his arms.

"Dinner tomorrow night."

"I can't. I already have plans."

"Oh?" Bart sounded surprised. His eyes twinkled in the soft light as if he were laughing at her.

"I do date, you know," Leanne said, getting angry at his apparent assumption that she didn't, and thankful that she had accepted Stephen's invitation. She couldn't have Bart thinking the way her parents did. But knowing the way he felt about Stephen, she couldn't very well tell him who was taking her out either. He would just have to believe her.

"I never doubted that you had dates. I'm sure you get lots of invitations. I was just under the impression that you didn't accept them." The music stopped and Leanne freed herself of his hold, skating to the carpeted area.

She thought that he would follow her, but instead he continued skating, playing chase with the children. They organized a snake of skaters and whizzed around the rink. Bart broke loose to help a little girl who had fallen down. He lifted her in his strong arms and whispered something in her ear. She giggled and he stood her gingerly on the floor, holding both her hands as he skated backward, pulling her along.

Tears came to Leanne's eyes as she watched him. There was so much about him that was right, but she was so afraid of being hurt. Did she dare take the chance? she thought, watching Bart come toward her. Quickly she turned her face so he couldn't see the tears.

"I didn't mean to upset you," he whispered as he covered her hand tenderly with his.

"I'm not upset," Leanne said, turning to face him with a quivering smile on her thin lips. "I'll be free *next* Friday night; what about you?"

Bart squeezed her hand gently and nodded his head. "Yes, I'll be free. I'll call you Monday about the time."

"You don't have my number."

"Your father . . ." Bart began, then laughed at the face Leanne had made.

"Of course. Dear Dad never gives up!"

"I'm glad he doesn't!" Bart said, winking before joining the children again.

Leanne tossed and turned all night, finally getting up. She might as well be doing something if she couldn't sleep, she thought, putting the teakettle on. She slid into a kitchen chair. This time last week, Bart and the boys were banging on her door. How mad she had been, she thought, absently pulling her fingers through her hair. She was thankful to her father, after all. For once his meddling had paid off. She just hoped she would still be thanking him when Bart decided to sweep someone else off her feet. The whistling of the teakettle interrupted her thoughts, and after making a cup of instant coffee, she went out on the deck.

In the hazy gray of dawn she could make out the outline of trees across the stream as the crisp spring air caused her to pull her robe close around her. Would Bart be out today? she wondered as she settled in a lounge chair. She lay her head back, setting her cup on a nearby table and gazing into the sky absently. The last things she remembered were the soft pink clouds that hovered over the hills.

Hearing voices, Leanne awoke with a jolt. The sun was high and glaring down in her sleepy eyes.

"Halt, soldier."

She recognized Charlie's authoritative voice, and through the trees she saw Mathew jerk to attention. They were playing army, and she felt privileged to watch them undetected. Her enjoyment was short-lived, however; soon she heard their father call them and watched the boys running away from her. She longed to join them, to be a part of their day, but she had to remind herself that they were a family and they needed time alone together.

Leanne placed her small hands on her jeans-clad hips, staring at the disarray of furniture in the living room while her foot tapped out her frustration. Now what? she thought, tucking a loose strand of hair back into the red bandanna that covered her head. The living room had been arranged and rearranged, but still she wasn't satisfied. Her small house had been begging for a spring cleaning, and as it seemed like a good way to get Bart off her mind, she had plunged into the work wholeheartedly.

As her hands moved the cloth against the window-panes she saw the shimmering stream through the streaks of window cleaner. There was the old log bridge Bart had carried her across. Leanne pictured his tall, lean frame on the water's edge, his hazel eyes smiling the way they always did. Blinking, she shook her head and turned from the window. This was terrible! How could she go all day knowing he was so close?

The day was agonizingly long, but finally it was late enough for her to start getting ready for her date with Stephen. She lingered in the bath for nearly an hour, then hurriedly slipped into burgundy slacks, tucking in her pink blouse. She covered her stockinged feet with black wedge heels before dashing a bit of color on her lips. She had just finished combing her hair when Stephen arrived.

"Hi," he said when she opened the door, the wind lifting his sandy brown hair. "Are you ready?"

"Let me get my bag." Leanne turned from the door and grabbed her purse off the couch.

As he pulled the sleek Jaguar onto the highway that led to town Leanne studied him. He was a nice-looking man, immaculately dressed, his chocolate sports shirt reminding her of the color of his eyes, his tan slacks neatly pressed, with a sharp crease. He wasn't much taller than she, but he was not a short man like her father.

"Has it been that long since you've seen me?" he asked, turning to glance at her.

"I'm sorry, Stephen," she said, unable to explain that she was comparing him with another man.

"I hope you won't mind, but the movie you wanted to see is sold out, so I bought tickets to a comedy instead. You look like you could use a good laugh. Something wrong?" he asked, pulling the car off the highway.

"No, not really. I've just been down a little," she answered, glancing out the window beside her so he couldn't see her face.

"Does it have anything to do with that guy that was on the creek bank when we left?"

"What guy?" Leanne turned quickly, her voice filled with surprise. She hadn't seen Bart. What was he doing there? she wondered. Had he recognized Stephen?

"There was some guy sitting across the creek staring, and he didn't look too happy to me. I heard your father sold that property. You already have trouble with your new neighbors?"

"Of course not." She laughed.

Stephen maneuvered the car into a parking place at the cinema. He was teasing her. The thought made her appreciate their easygoing friendship. She had known him when he spent his time in bars and came to work red-eyed and cranky because of a hangover. He had come to her the night of his conversion and poured his heart out. She had stood beside him when no one else would, and they had been close friends ever since. She had been able to receive comfort from him when Eric had left, and now she wanted to talk with him about Bart. But how could she, after what Bart had said about his sister?

After the movie, they stopped for coffee. As the waitress served them Leanne thought of how much Stephen had changed and wondered if he could have ever been the cad Bart had thought him to be. "Why haven't you ever married, Stephen?" she heard herself ask.

Stephen chuckled and stared into his cup. "I guess I spent too much time in a bottle trying to forget the one who got away and what I had become. . . . Someday I'll see her again." He was talking to himself, and Leanne felt as if she were intruding on his thoughts, but she wondered if he was referring to Linda.

They drove home in silence. Leanne felt guilty for the mood she had set. Leaning back in the velour-covered seat, she watched the stars above her through the open sunroof. The evening had started out light-hearted with the comedy they had seen, but it had ended on a rather melancholy note. In order to make amends for her folly, Leanne brought up the subject of some new merchandise she had seen at a recent showing, continuing their conversation long after Stephen had pulled into her drive and shut off the engine.

"It's quality merchandise, and I'm sure it will sell," Leanne said, leaning over to touch the light on his digital watch. "I'd better get in," she said, reaching for the door handle.

"See you Monday," Stephen said before she shut the car door. He started the engine and waited until she was inside before backing out the drive. She locked the door behind her, dropped her purse and keys onto the table, then got a soft drink out of the refrigerator. She sat at the table in the dark, staring out the bay window and wondering if Bart and the boys had stayed the night. She couldn't see a campfire; so, if they had, they were already asleep. Leanne watched a firefly near the stream. It was moving awfully slow, she thought. Suddenly the glow seemed to brighten as it hovered in midair before picking up speed and landing in the water.

"That was no firefly!" she said, standing and moving closer to the window. "That was a cigarette!" Bart's cigarette! Why was he there? she wondered. Had he been waiting for her to come home? How dare he spy on her! Furious, Leanne left the window and prepared for bed, knowing she would get little sleep.

Leanne ran the brush through her hair one more time before scooping it up on top of her head. She fastened it securely with needlelike ornaments. The week had been a long, arduous one, each day passing slowly. Mathew and Charlie had surprised her when they attended her Sunday school class, but she was disappointed at not seeing Bart at church. When he picked them up afterward, he had seemed in a hurry, barely acknowledging her before speeding away. She slipped into a shirtwaist dress, its flaming red color adding a glow to her cheeks. Bart had called later in the week to say he'd pick her up at seven, but he had seemed cool. He must have recognized Stephen. Could he be angry with her for dating him? Why else had he waited for her to come in that night? she thought, fastening the cloth-covered buttons that ran up the front of her dress.

Leanne fidgeted nervously with the straps of her bone sandal heels. She viewed her reflection in the mirror, running her hands over the jersey material of the full skirt. She made featherlike strokes at the wisps of hair that fell across her forehead, her eyes bright with anticipation. Would he be angry?

The doorbell rang, jolting her. Well, she would soon find out. She hesitated, closing her eyes and praying before opening the door. This was it. A night alone with the man who could make her lose sight of everything around her but his nearness. Don't leave me alone with him, God. I don't know how to handle the feelings he stirs. The doorbell sounded again, and she opened her eyes as well as the door.

Bart stood with his back to her, turning around as he heard the door open. His hazel eyes took on a grayish cast from his soft blue shirt, giving him the appearance of a stranger. However, as he arched a dark brow and whistled low, she knew he was the same Bart who had swept her off her feet.

"Is this the right house?" he asked teasingly, stepping back and pretending to look for a house number. "What happened to the little girl with the ponytail and jeans who used to live here?" Leanne blushed as he added, "Looks like I have a lovely woman on my hands tonight." He moved closer to cup her face in his hands. "You look beautiful," he said, his breath warm against her skin.

"You aren't really hungry, are you?" he asked, his low voice insinuating he had better ideas for the evening.

"Yes, I'm famished, in fact," she said, pulling out of his arms.

"Ah, still my innocent angel." His eyes sparkled with merriment as he pulled her back into his arms. "That's all right; I like innocent angels, as well as beautiful women."

She was breathless when he released her. "What about starving angels?" she asked playfully, shoving him out the door.

"Where are we going?" she inquired as he turned onto the highway.

"Are you sure you don't already know?" he replied, taking in the mandarin collar of her dress and the ornaments in her hair.

"How could I?" she asked, puzzled.

"Well, it's a secret," he said, glancing at her and winking before returning his attention to the road. "But I promise you'll enjoy it."

Of that I'm sure, she thought, comparing the earthy interior of the truck to Stephen's Jaguar. The two men were so different, one handsomely rugged and the other always looking as if he had stepped out of a tailor's shop. Leanne was surprised at the sudden change of outlook she had about Stephen. She had always appreciated his good taste in clothes and his immaculate appearance. But when compared with Bart, he seemed lacking.

Leanne was delighted when Bart pulled into the parking lot of the Paper Dragon, one of Tulsa's most exclusive restaurants. Now she understood why he thought she knew where they were going. A valet parked the car while they entered the restaurant through a courtyard. Two stone dragons guarded the entrance, and Leanne felt as though she had walked into another world. The gray walls outside had hidden the beauty of soft paper partitions and rain forests.

The maître d' led them past tables isolated by paper screens painted with colorful fire-breathing dragons. The soft pink lighting created an atmosphere for lovers. Leanne's heart raced at the anticipation of being alone with Bart in such a romantic setting, and she was relieved when the maître d' didn't stop but led them through another doorway into a more spacious area where tables were set for six instead of two. It was at one of these tables that he placed Leanne and Bart. Leanne smiled at the other couples at their table as Bart helped her with her chair.

A large Oriental man, dressed all in white and wearing a tall chef's hat, rolled a cart laden with knives, fresh meat, and vegetables in front of their horseshoe-shaped table. Leanne and Bart sat directly opposite a grill, with each of the other couples on either side of them. Her eyes widened as the man began to hit the sharp blades against one another, occasionally tossing one into the air and catching it miraculously by the handle. She turned eyes full of excitement to catch Bart watching her, not the cook. Unashamed, he held her gaze.

A bright flame suddenly burst into the air, drawing their attention as the chef threw brandy over the beef cubes, once more sending a blaze of color into the air. Bart watched Leanne, delighting in her excitement when the man flipped pieces of shrimp, beef and vegetables accurately onto each plate. Her eyes were still wide with amazement long after he had gone and they had begun to eat.

Afterward, while she relaxed in the car, she watched Bart as oncoming cars shed light on his face. The meal had been delicious and the atmosphere awesome. Bart had been attentive, watching her quietly all evening, occasionally taking her hand to his lips and causing her to blush in the presence of the other couples. He had acted as if she were his alone. Even now his hand covered hers possessively. Hadn't he called her *his* innocent angel before they had left? Fear gripped her at the thought of another possessive man taking over her life, making her dependent on him as Eric had, then leaving her. She had learned, the hard way, how to pick up the pieces, and she'd promised herself it would never happen again.

The truck pulled into the drive, and as Leanne reached for the door handle she felt Bart's grip on her hand tighten.

"Wait," he said, opening his door. He came around to her side to help her out.

"This isn't necessary for a liberated woman," Leanne said, smiling as she accepted his hand.

"It is for a liberated man," Bart said huskily, a protective arm around her as they walked toward the house, the shells crunching beneath their feet. As he turned the key in the lock Leanne wondered if he would expect to come in, not sure what she would do if he did. He handed her the keys and watched her methodically place them in her purse.

"Good night, Bart," she said, staring at his collar, afraid to meet his eyes. Afraid of what might be written there.

"Leanne." He spoke her name in a whisper, taking her hands in his and pulling her closer to him.

"I had a wonderful time," she said, her eyes riveted now on the dark wiry hairs of his chest. "I haven't enjoyed myself so much in a long time."

"Not even with Carlile?" he asked, bringing her hands to his shoulders and placing his at her waist. Leanne felt her breathing become ragged as he kissed her lightly, tormenting her senses. "Well?" he asked, his voice low and demanding.

Leanne was spellbound. "No," she whispered against his full lips, aching for the kiss they promised.

"Then you've no reason to see him again," he commanded.

"What?" she asked, pulling away. What she had feared was coming true!

"After seeing you with Carlile, I think your father is right. You need a man to look after you," he said, not allowing her out of the circle of his arms.

"You and my father are crazy!" Leanne said angrily, straining to free herself of his hold. "I don't need two men trying to run my love life."

"If Carlile's the best you can do, then you need *someone* to handle it for you," he said, a deep rumble sounding in his chest as he laughed, holding her against him, easily ignoring her struggles.

"Charles Bartholomew Hall, you are hopeless!" Leanne protested.

"I know," he said, kissing her parted lips tenderly before releasing her and walking away.

It wasn't he that was hopeless, Leanne thought, watching his taillights until they disappeared. It was the whole situation. Eric, too, had put demands on her, and she had allowed it then; but she had learned her lesson, and she would not allow it now.

Chapter Four

Leanne thought all night of some way to prove to Bart that she would see Stephen if she wanted to. Of course, she could continue to date him, and she wanted Bart to *know* that she had defied him. By morning, she was exhausted and still had not thought of an adequate plan. After shuffling through her usual routine of housework, Leanne decided to work with her plants. It was a beautiful, warm day, and as she loved to work with her hands, there was nothing more relaxing.

As a result of the spring-cleaning she had done the week before, there were plants scattered all over the redwood deck. Some just needed a good bath, while others required a larger pot. She sprayed the wide green leaves of a philodendron with the water hose and was beginning to repot the bromeliad her mother had named Sophie when Bart pulled into her drive.

"Looks like you've got a jungle started here!" Bart said, slamming the truck door.

Leanne looked up to see him smiling at her through the spiny leaves of a Chinese fan palm. "What are you doing here?" she asked, continuing to work with Sophie.

"After last night, I thought you would be glad to see me," he teased, leaning forward against the deck, watching her.

Leanne ignored his remark and brushed the soil from her hands before reaching for the hose. When she pulled the trigger to spray the plant, no water came forth. Twisting the water gun sideways, she examined the mechanism. Suddenly water spewed out, drenching Bart. Laughing wildly at his startled look, Leanne watched his expression turn from surprise to mischief, and she found herself holding the nozzle of the hose toward him in self-defense as she backed away from the deck cautiously. Bart slowly rounded the corner of the redwood platform, coming toward her, ignoring her trivial weapon.

"Bart, I warn you . . ." But her warning came too late as he suddenly pounced on her, grabbing the end of the hose as she ran in the opposite direction, screaming when the cold water splashed across the back of her khaki shirt.

Hiding behind the safety of a large oak tree near the creek, Leanne peeked out to find that Bart had dropped the hose and was nowhere in sight. A frown creased her brow as she searched the yard for his tall frame. Where could such a large man be hiding? she thought, stooping to see under the deck. Before she could stand again, strong fingers gripped her waist and rolled her to the soft ground, tickling her until she begged for mercy. He imprisoned her arms against the ground above her head and leaned over her.

Leanne tried to regain her breath, but the smile in his eyes made it difficult. She had been so angry with him only minutes before; yet now her arms ached to hold him. She waited for him to kiss her, but instead, he released her and sat with his back against the trunk of the tree.

Leanne lay there staring at the Oklahoma sky, watching white clouds form odd shapes against a blue background. Her dark hair lay in a spray across the green grass and her cutoff jeans revealed slender tan legs and bare feet.

Bart is such a puzzle, she thought. One minute taking her into his arms, being considerate and gentle; the next so nonchalant and arrogant. She was a fool to allow herself to get involved with him. She should never have allowed him to walk her home from her parents' house that first night. Nibbling at the corner of her lower lip, she remembered what fun she had had with him and his children these past few weeks. Already they were too much a part of her life to just forget them.

The click of Bart's cigarette lighter attracted her attention, and Leanne moved her head to the side, watching his eyes become narrow slits as the smoke hovered around his face before dispersing. His full lips stretched across his rugged face as he smiled, causing her to avert her gaze.

"That's a bad habit you have," she said, watching a squirrel scamper across a bough above her.

Bart raised an eyebrow. "I know," he said, looking thoughtfully at the cigarette in his hand before flicking the ashes off. "But it's the *only* bad habit I have," he added with a grin.

A half smile curved Leanne's mouth. A typical answer, she thought. A hush fell across them and Leanne closed her eyes to Bart's study of her. A gentle breeze rustled the large leaves overhead. Breathing deeply, she caught the smell of tobacco mingled with the fresh smell of grass and soil. Unconsciously, Leanne clenched her fists. She couldn't even breathe without Bart entering her thoughts.

"Are you free this evening?" he asked, leaning forward. His arms rested across the top of his bent knees as he drew on the cigarette. Leanne couldn't be alone with him again. He was too confident, too possessive and above all, too desirable.

"Where are Mathew and Charlie?" she asked.

"Visiting their aunt. And your plans?" he asked again.

"I'm expecting Stephen to call."

"I thought you'd forgotten me."

Leanne heard Stephen's voice behind her. She jerked to a sitting position, opening her eyes to the sharp crease of his navy slacks as he came toward them.

"I thought I'd bring these over so you could see the figures for yourself," he said as he handed her a brown folder. "My name's Stephen Carlile." He introduced himself to Bart, extending his hand as he did so.

Bart dropped his cigarette at his feet, grinding it out with the heel of his boot before accepting the handshake. "Bart Hall," he said, watching with pleasure as Stephen's face paled with recognition.

Leanne jumped to her feet. "I'm glad you're here, Stephen," she said, though she had hoped to avoid this confrontation.

"Yes, we were just talking about you," Bart added.

"Stephen and I are going to Tahlequah to see the Indian village this evening," she said, curling her hand around Stephen's arm. "Aren't we, Stephen?" she asked, her fingers applying pressure, urging him to read between the lines.

Stephen glanced quickly down at Bart, then back to Leanne. "Oh, sure . . . sure."

"I'd better get ready," Leanne said, moving toward the house. "We'll have to be leaving soon."

"Yeah, that's a long drive," Stephen said with a sigh as he ran a hand through his sandy hair, obviously not looking forward to the trip.

"Why don't you let me fly you?" Bart asked. Leanne stopped and turned around, shooting him a blazing glare. Ignoring her angry look, he added, "Then you'll have time for the steaks that I brought." Bart stood, his legs apart, his hands set loosely in his jeans pockets. He smiled, proud of the way he was including himself in her plans with Stephen.

"You fly?" Leanne looked at him doubtfully.

Bart laughed at the disbelief on her face. "I've been flying for years."

"You have your own plane?" Stephen asked curiously.

"Yes. It's faster and much more relaxing than fighting the crowds at airports."

"Bart," Leanne began as she stepped forward, "I—"

"You aren't afraid of my flying, are you?" Bart

interrupted her, daring her to object to his going with them.

"No, it's not that. I—we—" she stuttered, feeling trapped.

"You've got to admit a twenty-minute flight is better than an hour-and-a-half drive, right, Carlile?"

"I guess I can't argue with that," Stephen replied eagerly.

Leanne looked from one man to the other. Stephen shrugged his shoulders and Bart smiled. "Then it's settled. I'll get the charcoal started," he said, walking toward his truck. "Help me with the steaks, Carlile?"

Stephen looked helplessly toward Leanne before following Bart. Furious, she stomped her bare foot, her hands on her hips and her mouth a tight, thin line across her face as she watched the two men walk away. She couldn't believe it! Bart had just intruded on her plans whether she liked it or not, and Stephen hadn't even had the courage to stand up to him.

Fuming, Leanne stormed up the slope toward the house. If Stephen only knew, she thought, pushing her hair away from her face, remembering Bart's words of the night before. He was determined to keep her from dating Stephen, and it looked as though he would have his way despite her feelings. Leanne slowed her pace, resignedly. She would just have to keep her temper in check until she could get Bart alone.

Leanne finished repotting her plants while Bart and Stephen discussed the starting baseball season. Bart occasionally checked on the steaks and the small potato halves he had wrapped in foil and dropped into the coals. When the food was done, Leanne added a salad, and they ate the savory meal at the patio table on the deck. Though the conversation was strained, they soon finished with their dinner, and Leanne changed while Bart and Stephen cleared the table.

Alone in her bedroom, Leanne decided to take her time getting ready. It would serve Bart right to have to make polite conversation with Stephen. He seemed capable so far, though Leanne knew it was only to spite her. Stephen was acting as if they were old friends, so she didn't worry about him.

After tugging on her western boots, Leanne tucked her jeans inside them and stood to survey her reflection. The cream cotton blouse with capped sleeves was decorated by tiny embroidered flowers at the yoke, and the wooden beads she wore added authenticity to her outfit. Her shiny hair lay in dark waves about her face and shoulders. Her green eyes sparkled and she felt pleased with herself. Dropping her keys into her canvas shoulder bag, she joined the men outside.

"You look great," Stephen said, rising from his chair as she closed the door behind her.

"Thank you, Stephen," she replied, glancing at Bart and blushing at his quiet appraisal of her figure.

"Are we ready?" Bart asked, getting to his feet.

"Leanne?" Stephen looked at her quizzically.

"Yes, I'm ready," she replied.

"I'll move my car," Stephen said as he walked toward his Jaguar, parked behind Bart's truck.

Leanne looked at Bart through squinted eyes, and when Stephen was out of hearing range, she voiced her pent-up anger. "You think you're pretty smart, don't you, Bart Hall?"

"What do you mean?" Bart watched her as he lit a cigarette and blew the smoke slowly, irritating her.

Leanne waved her hand to clear the air before she spoke again. "You know what I mean! How dare you invite yourself to go on another man's date? My plans were with Stephen, not you!"

"I have no intentions of moving in on Carlile's . . . date with you. I simply offered my services as chauffeur and pilot." Bart smiled innocently, getting into the truck and starting the engine.

On the drive to the airport, Leanne's stomach was filled with butterflies. Just to be sitting close to Bart was intoxicating. *How did I get mixed up in this charade?* she wondered as they made their way down winding roads, finally turning into a long drive that ran between miles of open field. In the distance Leanne could see a large metal barn. As they moved closer small airplanes came into view and the high fields gave way to a wide landing strip. Bart parked near the hangar and got out, leaving Stephen and Leanne to follow.

"Good to see you, Mr. Hall," a tall, lanky man in coveralls said when they entered the hangar. He wiped the grease off his hands onto the old rag he held. "Haven't seen you in a while."

"Well, Doug, I've been pretty busy these last weeks." Bart moved aside and, looking from Leanne and Stephen back to the hangar attendant, added, "This is Leanne Masterson and Stephen Carlile. I'm going to give them a lift to the Cherokee village near Tahlequah. Is Tandra ready for a short run?" He walked farther into the hangar, with the attendant close behind him.

"Yes, sir. I've been starting her up every other day just to keep her in tune. Plenty of gas and waiting to see you."

Leanne and Stephen followed the two men through the hangar, passing several small planes, Leanne thinking each one would be Tandra. When they reached the back of the hangar, the attendant opened a large sliding door, revealing a metallic blue helicopter with shiny silver blades, a colorful silhouette against the darkening Oklahoma sky. Leanne had never flown in a helicopter before, and though it was a beautiful aircraft, she wasn't sure she wanted to now.

"Bart, I thought you meant a plane . . . not a . . ." Leanne stuttered.

"Chopper?" Bart finished for her, smiling. "There's nothing to be afraid of," he assured her.

"I don't think I want to," Leanne said, backing away from Bart before he could maneuver her toward the helicopter.

Stephen was fascinated with the idea and had already approached the aircraft. "It's going to be fun, Leanne," he said, stepping back to take in Tandra's full height and long blades.

Leanne had counted on Stephen's support, but it didn't look as though he were going to be of any help to her. Reluctantly she climbed into the rear seat of the egg-shaped vehicle, and Stephen got in next to her. Bart checked her safety belt, his face close to hers as he leaned across her. A smile sparkled in his hazel eyes. How handsome he was, and how utterly arrogant! He hadn't wanted her to see Stephen again, and her plan to oppose him had backfired. The strange part about it was that she was glad.

Bart started the engine, and Leanne cringed as she heard the blades begin to whir overhead. Through the large bubbled glass at her side Leanne watched Doug's coveralls whip around his thin frame while he held his cap to his head and waved. Suddenly she felt the helicopter sway, then lift smoothly off the ground, carrying them over the wide fields of tall grass, which flattened with the strong wind. Bart pulled a lever and the vehicle rose into the air, slanting to one side as he maneuvered a turn. Leanne was so taken with the view of the sunset in front of her that she forgot her fear and began to relax.

It was dark when they reached the village and Bart lowered the helicopter into a nearby field, creating a spectacle for the tourists and locals alike. As they disembarked, however, the crowds turned back to the open fires where iron rotisseries turned roasts and chickens near rawhide tepees. When they approached the village, Leanne saw several Indian men sitting cross-legged in their buckskin pants as they passed around a long wooden pipe painted with colorful stripes and carved designs. Farther along there were women with long dark braids cooking and tending to the necessities of the upcoming feast. Though she had been to the village often, Leanne still marveled at its atmosphere.

They moved along the circle of tents, and as they were watching a group of young women stringing colorful wooden beads to make the jewelry they had displayed on soft animal skins, Leanne realized that Bart had left her with Stephen, disappearing into the crowds of tourists that meandered through the village. Instantly she felt an empty feeling invade her senses. The bright colors faded and the voices around her blended together, becoming meaningless without Bart to share them. He had kept his word; he was not interfering with her date with Stephen.

Chapter Five

Leanne threw her burgundy swimsuit into the suitcase, wishing she had bought a new one this year. Her trip to Tahlequah with Bart and Stephen had taken place over three weeks ago. Since then, Bart had won her confidence again, though she couldn't understand how. "He could charm a refrigerator right out the door," Leanne said as she shut the case and snapped the latch. She smiled as she recalled how desperately she had wanted him instead of Stephen by her side that night at the Indian village. After he had disappeared, she and Stephen had visited a witch doctor's tent and examined the detail of a hand-carved totem pole, and when they had been served their plates of roasted chicken and stewed vegetables, they had joined the other tourists seated on straw mats that formed a circle around a brilliant fire to watch the Indian dance. Stephen had been too caught up in the ritual to notice her constant surveying of the crowd. Once, as she had watched the dancers in their colorful feather head-dresses and beads, she saw Bart outside the circle, leaning against the totem pole.

Leanne yawned as she carried the suitcase and her overnight bag to the living room. She glanced at her watch. It was after five in the morning, and Bart had said he would pick her up before then. Staring out the window into the darkness, she wondered what was keeping him.

They had dated several times during the past few weeks, Leanne unconsciously making excuses to avoid Stephen. Her vacation time had arrived and Bart had offered to take her to Galveston, Texas, for the day. She had laughed when he suggested it. "Not in your helicopter, I hope!"

"No," he had said. "In my plane!" She had been taken aback to think he owned both, and had said so. "Actually, the plane belongs to the company, but it is at my disposal," he had explained.

Suddenly a soft light fell across the road, and she knew it was caused by the headlights of Bart's truck. Soon the light grew brighter and she watched him pull into the drive. She flipped on the porch light and excitedly rushed out the door to meet him with a warm kiss.

"Sorry to be late," he said, still holding her in his arms. "There was a mix-up about the plane, but it's taken care of. Are you ready?" he asked, moving toward the house, his arm across her shoulders.

"Mm-hm," Leanne murmured, brushing her face against the powerful hand that dangled at her shoulder. How she loved the feel of him close to her, his strong arms holding her, compelling her to trust him, which was exactly what she had grown to do. She had never felt this way about Eric, about anyone. Yet something kept her from revealing her feelings to him.

Bart put her bags into the truck and they drove to the airport. The hangar attendant recognized Leanne and amazed her by remembering her name. "Good morning, Mr. Hall. Nice to see you again, Miss Masterson. Going to Texas, I understand."

Leanne smiled. "Yes. Bart has offered to show me Galveston Beach."

"Never been there myself, though I've seen some beautiful beaches from the air," the man said. Bart helped Leanne onto the wing of the Cessna 310 and into the cabin. "You guys have a good time," Doug called to them through the open door.

"We plan to," Bart replied, smiling contagiously at Leanne before slamming the door and settling into the pilot's seat. She watched excitedly as he hit a switch, then punched a red button that started one of the engines. After he started the second engine, they began to taxi down the runway. Leanne held her breath as the aircraft began to rise gently higher and higher into the dark sky. She watched the lights below her slowly fade as they climbed still higher, passing through a cloud.

"Happy?" Bart asked, glancing her way.

"Very." She turned to flash him a smile.

Bart watched the instrument panel in front of him; then, snapping on the autopilot, he leaned back, allowing the electronic circuitry to take over his job while he briefed Leanne on their itinerary for the day.

Time passed quickly, and soon Bart took control of the plane again, using the radio to inform the airport in

Galveston of their approach. "You love the sunrise, don't you?" Bart asked, watching the delight on her face. The shoreline came into view and a large orange ball peeked over the edge, casting pink and purple colors across the soft clouds, the hues of the sun reflecting on the water.

Seated in a taxi, Leanne and Bart left Stewart Field to travel down a winding road that the driver assured them bypassed the town and led directly to the beach. Leanne watched the road in front of them dip, and as the car mounted the slope she gasped. A wide expanse of aqua water stretched for miles in front of them. The driver turned onto the road that ran along the top of the seawall and was appropriately named Seawall Boulevard. A wide sidewalk followed the road at the edge of the wall and was landscaped with tall palm trees encircled by benches at intervals on the wall.

"There's a lot to see and do here on the island," Bart said, kissing her lightly. "Not counting the surprise I have for you. But first, we'll get breakfast and change into our suits at the hotel." Leanne's green eyes twinkled excitedly. Together they watched the tourist attractions as their taxi sped toward the hotel. Leanne felt eager for the surprise Bart had promised.

Soon the cab turned into a circular drive in front of a large stucco building. A red canvas-covered walkway extended to the center of the driveway, and it was here that the driver stopped. Leanne stood on the sidewalk while Bart paid the cab fare and got their luggage. She was enchanted by the round veranda to her right that held dining tables with bright red tablecloths, and she watched as waiters in red jackets and black slacks brought coffee to the customers who sat enjoying the sea breeze as well as the clear view of the ocean.

She turned to Bart and, taking her small bag from him, she said, "You didn't rent a room here just for us to change in?"

"Why not?" he asked, throwing his hanging bag over his shoulder and grabbing up her suitcase. "Only the best for you. It isn't often that I am entrusted with the care of an angel, you know? Allow me at least the privilege of showering you with a little luxury," he said, teasing.

Leanne blushed and walked with him into the hotel; but as they approached the U-shaped desk, a sudden dread filled her. Would Bart take two rooms?

While they waited for another couple to sign the register, Leanne surveyed the lobby. It was a beautiful hotel. The rooms were sure to be expensive. Oh Lord, she prayed silently, what am I doing here? A lump rose in her throat and she swallowed back the threat of tears. Bart squeezed her hand gently and smiled. Leanne returned a quivering smile, then averted her gaze to study the pattern of the carpet. He's going to laugh at me when I insist on two rooms, she thought.

"Can I help you?" The clerk finally asked Bart.

"Yes," she heard Bart say. "You have reservations for Bart Hall?"

"Let's see."

Leanne watched the clerk run his finger down a column and when he lifted his head she held her breath and prayed Bart would understand.

"Here we are, rooms three twenty and three twenty one."

Leanne sighed with relief.

"Something wrong?" Bart asked her.

Leanne took his arm. "Not a thing," she answered, relief evident on her face.

"Your keys, sir." The clerk handed Bart two keys and a bellman took their bags up.

Alone in the elevator, Bart leaned against the wall and watched Leanne, a mischievous smile on his face. "Did I do the right thing?" he asked. "You looked as if you were a bit nervous back there."

Leanne looked into his eyes. Was he laughing at her after all? "What do you mean?" she asked innocently as she watched the numbers light up above the elevator doors. The doors opened and Leanne glanced at Bart before stepping out. His expression had changed and the look in his eyes was sincere.

"Never mind," he said, shaking his head and hugging her against his side. "Let's change and have some coffee before we explore the deep sea."

Leanne changed into the one-piece burgundy swimsuit she had brought. Slipping on a short white terrycloth cover-up and a pair of sandals, she opened her door and found Bart waiting in the hallway. He wore camel-colored trunks with a blue stripe on each side that matched the blue cotton shirt he had left open down the front, revealing his tanned chest, covered with dark hair that ran from his throat down to his lean waist. He was terribly handsome, she thought.

Bart picked up the beach bag at his feet. "I thought that after breakfast we'd take a walk up the beach. Are you game?" he asked, placing his free arm across her shoulders and directing her toward the elevator.

"I'm game for most anything today!" she exclaimed happily.

They ate a simple breakfast of rolls and coffee on the veranda before starting out. At the intersection in front of the hotel, Leanne and Bart waited while cars made their way slowly along the seawall, the passengers and drivers alike viewing the sights around them. When they had crossed the busy boulevard, Bart led her down cement steps to where sand stretched to meet blue water laced with white bubbles.

Bart had been holding Leanne's hand, but he released it promptly as he felt her need to be free. He watched her run to the edge of the water, then hop backward as the waves broke and rolled swiftly toward her feet. She turned to Bart, delight on her face as she ran toward him, throwing herself into his arms.

"I love it!" she cried, turning again to watch the rhythm of the water, her arm still at Bart's waist and his across her shoulders. They stood together, Bart watching Leanne's face, while her eyes were captured by the white-and-gray birds that soared above the water, dipping occasionally to catch a fish.

After strolling along the beach for a while, they walked out onto one of the long rock piers called jetties. Men and women were fishing or catching crabs. Leanne had never seen a crab and was fascinated by the stony-looking creatures. A man pulled one up with a net and dropped it onto the pier. When it scurried sideways toward Leanne, she shrieked, jumping behind Bart for protection. Bart set the beach bag on the pointed blue pincers and picked the crab up from behind, dropping it into the man's bucket. Several children scrambled down the pier, their mothers calling to them not to run. Bart placed a protective arm around Leanne just in time to keep her from tumbling backward into the water as the children, ignoring their mothers, ran past them.

They made their way back to the beach and Bart led her up the seawall steps to the boulevard. They had traveled several blocks, and now, instead of the hotel, they faced a row of shops sprinkled amid fast-food restaurants.

"How about some chicken?" Bart asked, his eyes dancing as they crossed the street.

"But we just ate," Leanne said, hopping up onto the curb before a stream of cars raced past her.

"I mean for lunch," he said as they reached the diner specializing in fried chicken.

Bart placed their order while Leanne found the ladies' room. When she returned, he was using the pay phone, adding to the mysterious mood he had set.

After paying for their meal, they took the white paper bag of chicken outside. A yellow cab was parked near the door, and Leanne knew Bart had called for it. The mystery deepened, and Leanne was filled with anticipation for the surprise she knew was to come.

As the cab made its way down the busy street Leanne watched tourists pedaling a surrey down the sidewalk next to them, the canvas top with its fringed edges keeping the now-hot sun off their heads. She turned excitedly to Bart, who was watching her. Before she could even ask, he answered, laughter in his eyes, "Of course we can rent one." The driver turned off the boulevard onto another street, taking them through town, then across a long bridge, stopping at a marina to let them out.

Leanne had never been sailing and was thrilled when Bart rented a sailboat, surprising her by taking them across the blue water to a private cove for a picnic. They docked the small boat near the shore and raced along the sand toward a clump of trees growing at the bottom of a high embankment.

Bart dug into the drawstring bag and took out a large beach towel, which he spread on the sand for them to sit on while they ate their feast. The salty air had made Leanne feel famished, and she was ready for the lunch Bart had bought. She used the paper plates supplied by the diner to serve the chicken and potato salad, feeling Bart's eyes on her all the while.

"When will the boys be back from summer camp?" she asked, handing Bart his plate.

"Not until Friday, which gives me exactly four days to come up with a housekeeper for them."

"A housekeeper?"

"Their grandmother has taken ill and won't be able to keep them for a few weeks, maybe longer." Bart set his plate on the sand behind him and took Leanne's from her lap. "But I didn't bring you out here to a secluded spot to talk about children and grandmothers." He leaned toward Leanne, only to have her jump to her feet, laughing, and run to the surf, shedding her cover-up as she went. Bart stood watching her splash into the water, his hands on his hips and a smile across his handsome face. Slowly he removed his shirt and tossed it onto the towel before chasing after her.

When he reached her, Bart dunked Leanne under the water; then, sliding his arms around her wet body, he pulled her up against him. The water had made her eyes sting, but the salty taste of Bart's kiss made her oblivious to all else.

When their lips parted, Leanne turned within the circle of his arms to lean her back against his chest. The water stretched before them, shimmering in the sunlight as it met the blue sky on the horizon. She had never been so happy. God had been so good to her, sending Bart into her life.

"Thank you Lord," she whispered, barely audible.

"Hmm?" Bart asked, leaning forward, his rough cheek brushing against hers.

Leanne snuggled against his warmth, feeling loved and protected. "I was just thinking how good God is."

"You think so?" Bart asked, relaxing his hold on her a little.

"Oh yes." Leanne laughed lightly. "He can take the worst possible situation and, if you trust Him to, He can make everything come out right. Just look at us," she teased.

But Bart was silent, as though he hadn't heard her last words. "Don't you agree?" Leanne asked, leaning her head back at an angle in order to see his face. His expression was unreadable as he stared into the distance.

"I would have agreed at one time. In fact, you'd be surprised," he added, glancing down at her. "But I don't know anymore." Bart looked away and Leanne followed his gaze to watch the sailboats now along the horizon in front of them.

"I can't imagine my life without Him," Leanne said softly as she turned around. Absently, Bart massaged the back of her neck while he studied her face intently. With her hand on his chest, Leanne could feel his heart beating rapidly. "It's really just a question of trust, Bart."

"That's your opinion, angel," he said with a sigh. "I wish I could share it," he added, his lips forming a smile that didn't reach his eyes. Letting her go, he dived into the water and swam away from her.

Leanne stood, aching to join him, but his strokes were hard and she knew he meant to be alone. She slowly waded back to the shore to wait for him there. After clearing the picnic supplies, she stretched out on the towel, closing her eyes and hoping to rid herself of the apprehension she felt.

The warm sun seared her skin and dried her hair before she finally heard Bart's approach. A fine shower of sand fell across her legs and she opened her eyes, turning to see Bart sitting at a distance from her. His arms rested on his bent knees, and a cigarette dangled from his firm lips.

"You smoke too much!" Leanne declared as she sat up, facing him and brushing the gritty sand from her skin.

"Maybe," he agreed, grinding the fire out in the sand. "But you snore," he teased, his eyes smiling once more.

"I do not!" Leanne said in mock defense. "I wasn't even asleep." She laughed. He was trying to recapture the lightheartedness they had shared earlier, and she welcomed a release of the tension she felt.

Bart began to build a sand castle and Leanne joined him, reveling in the peace they had made. The afternoon was still ahead of them, and she was glad that it wasn't going to be spent under a strain. They built a wonderful castle with a moat around it and a drawbridge made from a piece of driftwood Bart found near the trees.

After sailing back to the marina, they took a taxi to the seawall, where Bart rented a surrey, which they pedaled along the sidewalk. The passing teenagers on roller skates who whizzed around them reminded Leanne of the skating party Bart had gone to with her so long ago.

They pedaled several blocks; then, seeing that Leanne was getting tired, Bart returned the surrey to another rental house located farther down the seawall. "Do you want to get a cab back to the hotel and rest awhile before dinner?"

"What I would really like to do is walk back by way of the beach," she said pleadingly.

"Of course." Bart smiled, his eyes twinkling as he squinted them against the bright sun. They walked in silence down the beach, occasionally passing a family enjoying their vacation, or teenagers playing ball. Leanne collected shells along the water's edge and stuffed them into the beach bag to place in her aquarium when she returned home.

They passed several gift shops and stopped to browse, buying souvenirs for Mathew and Charlie, their grandmother and Leanne's parents. The last shop they encountered was selling hand-blown glass objects, and they watched the artist at work. Leanne was fascinated with the craft, but soon she ventured beyond the shop to a deck that overlooked the Gulf. Bart lingered to talk to the artist, joining her after a short time, and together they enjoyed the colors of the sun reflected on the water. A light breeze cooled her burning skin. There was a peaceful silence between them as they walked slowly back to the hotel.

Chapter Six

Locking the door behind her, Leanne slowly stripped out of the gritty bathing suit and stepped into the soothing flow of the shower. She couldn't forget the look in Bart's eyes when they had talked about trusting Christ. It had been a look of pain. But why? she wondered, as she poured shampoo onto her wet hair, rubbing it into a rich lather. She knew very little of Bart's past, but something or someone had caused him to turn against God. Hadn't he insinuated that at one time he had been closer to Him? Leanne thought of Bart's marriage to Carol. Had they worshiped together? Or had he lost his faith in Christ before he met her? Absently, Leanne played with the thick lather in her hands. It hurt to think of Bart with someone else. Mathew's and Charlie's freckled faces flashed into her mind and Leanne stepped under the water, rinsing the shampoo out of her hair and the growing jealousy out of her thoughts.

Carefully patting the beads of water off her sunburned skin, Leanne tried to remember that Carol, and she hoped any other woman that Bart had cared for, were in his past. It was Bart's past experience with Christ that was her real concern. She wrapped a thick towel around her head, turban-style, and securing a bath sheet above her small breasts, she moved into the adjoining bedroom.

Leanne opened the antique wardrobe to find the dress she had brought to wear to dinner. Placing the raspberry-colored garment on the bed, she went back into the bathroom, taking her blow dryer with her. "Lord," she called under her breath, "give me the opportunity to help Bart know your love again."

After drying her hair and slipping into the dress, she gingerly walked across the room toward the full-length mirror, her stockinged feet sinking into the thick carpet. Facing her reflection in the mirror, Leanne wondered if the peasant chemise would be appropriate for the restaurant Bart had chosen. The border print bottom matched the yokes, and as she tied the keyhole opening at the neck Leanne decided that at least the dress was loose-fitting and comfortable against her sunburn. Besides, she thought, smiling to herself, it's my only choice. Leanne slipped into her shoes and applied a touch of makeup to her flushed face. She parted her hair on the side, allowing its full soft waves to tumble down her back and lie loosely about her face.

Adjusting the full sleeves with elasticized cuffs, Leanne winced from the movement of the dress against her back. She was glad that the dress would cover her red skin so Bart wouldn't know how badly she had burned. She didn't feel like a beautiful woman tonight, but rather like a foolish child. It had been a long time since she'd been burned so severely. She knew she should have used tanning lotion, but there was no time to worry about that, as Bart was probably waiting for her in the hall now.

She was reaching for the doorknob when a knock sounded. Talk about timing, she thought, smiling to herself as she opened the door. Bart was giving a bellman a tip for a small package he had in his hand. Leanne's eyes widened as she caught sight of a bouquet of long-stemmed white roses that sat on the floor at the man's feet. The bellman left and Bart turned, the small package in his hands.

"Oh, you're finally through?" he teased, light dancing in his eyes as he came forward.

"What's that?" Leanne asked, referring to the package.

"This?" he asked nonchalantly. "This is for you. But not just yet," he added, his large hand covering the small box as his other hand touched her burning cheek. A look of concern crossed his face. "Too much sun today?"

"Not really. I'm used to being exposed to it. I'll be all right." Leanne turned toward the flowers. "They're lovely, Bart."

"I'm glad you like them. They suit you," he said, concern still edging his voice. Leanne bent to smell the velvety white folds, gritting her teeth against the pain the movement caused, glad her back was to Bart.

"Are you sure you're all right?" he asked as he picked up the flowers and helped her stand.

"I'm fine," Leanne said, forcing a smile. As they entered her room, the faint ringing of a telephone could be heard from across the hall. "You'd better answer your phone," she said, willing him to leave her alone for a few minutes. She didn't want him to discover her foolishness in not using tanning lotion, and if he didn't leave the room soon, he would surely find out.

Bart arranged the flowers and the package on the dressing table near her purse. "I'll only be a minute," he called over his shoulder, as he crossed the hall.

Leanne pulled the weight of her hair off her shoulders, sighing with the relief it brought. Resting as comfortably as possible in an armchair, she tried to rid her mind of the misery she was in. The soft scent of the roses caught her attention, and she smiled. Maybe he was impossible at times, but he knew how to win her heart with flowers. Her eyes were drawn to the small package on the stand. Gingerly she stood and walked to the Victorian-style table. Taking the small box in her hands, she examined it curiously, feeling like a child at Christmas. It was wrapped in glossy, white paper, with a silver bow tied around it. What could it possibly be? she wondered, turning the gift over in her palm. It was so small. Leanne gasped. Could it possibly be . . . ? No, she wouldn't let herself even think so. Yet, it was the size of a ring box. Leanne dropped the small package onto the glass-topped table. If it were an engagement ring, if he were to propose to her tonight, what would she say? Was she ready to make another commitment? Pacing the floor, Leanne forgot about her sunburn. Her pain was in her heart as she searched for an answer to her own question.

She was standing at the bay window overlooking the seawall and the blue water beyond it when she heard Bart enter the room. She turned to him nervously, facing his smiling eyes. He was so handsome. The wine and gray stripes against the white background of his dress shirt accented the ashen suit he wore. His eyes held hers and the dark lashes of one winked at her as a smile tugged at the corners of his full lips. How could she resist him?

Somewhere deep inside her a warning sounded. She had thought she couldn't resist Eric, too, and now she wished she had. What had happened to the trust she had begun to feel in Bart? The thought of being engaged again had made her toss all reason to the wind. Try as she might, she could think of nothing he had done to gain her confidence. Turning back to the window, she desperately tried to remember why she had trusted him, but her mind was a blank. All she could think of was the small white box lying innocently on the table, not yet guilty of ruining her whole life. If she told Bart no, she might never see him again, and that she couldn't bear; but if she accepted his proposal, she might be letting herself in for another bitter heartbreak that would only leave her lonely and withdrawn.

Bart's breath was warm on her neck, startling her. "Did I tell you how beautiful you look?" he asked. His hand, moving into the dark waves of her hair, sent a thrilling chill over her and compelled her to face him.

Leanne gazed deep into his dancing eyes, searching for his true feelings. Did he love her? All she saw was a reflection of her own confused emotions. She had to keep her senses; she had to know he loved her. If he didn't, then there was nothing worthwhile to their relationship.

"What time did you make our reservations for?" she asked before his lips touched hers, muffling her words. She placed her hands on his chest and gently pushed him, urging him to let her go.

He glanced at his watch. "I guess it is about that time, isn't it?" Taking her hand in his, he led her toward the door, stopping to pick up her purse and the white box. Leanne's heart raced as she watched him reach for it. She couldn't open it, not yet. But he handed her the purse and tucked the box into his pocket as they walked into the hallway, Bart locking the door behind them.

Twenty minutes later, their taxi let them out in front of a two-story plantation home with tall white columns. Leanne pushed her worries to the back of her mind, determined not to allow anything to spoil the evening, as it might prove to be her last with Bart. She would put off opening the gift until they had returned to Tulsa, no matter how persistent he became.

They entered the renovated home that now served as a restaurant. The wide foyer was lit softly with wall sconces that flickered, causing shadows to dance on the glossy sheen of the polished hardwood floor. Huge paintings hung on the dark paneled walls between the sconces, and a grouping of furniture covered with blue satin brocade made an impressive waiting area. However, they didn't have to wait. A young woman dressed in a full-length ballroom gown greeted them.

"Good evening," she said, a cascade of curls bouncing at her shoulders as she bent to pick up her skirt. "This way, Mr. Hall."

Leanne looked curiously up at Bart, who took her small hand and placed it in the crook of his arm. "What can I say?" he whispered near her ear. "I dine here often."

With whom? Leanne wondered, the green monster rising in her thoughts again. This wasn't the type of place one had business meetings.

As they traveled down the long hall Leanne noted the antiques that decorated each room they passed. When they came to the ballroom entrance, Leanne felt transported back in time as she stopped to watch the guests at a costume party, dressed in colonial fashion, dance to violin music provided by the small orchestra set up in a corner.

Bart patted her hand and led her across the foyer to the back of the house, where they followed the hostess up a wide staircase that could have been used in the shooting of *Gone With the Wind*. The banister was carved of heavy oak and the wide steps were carpeted with an Oriental print done in blue and burgundy and accented with gold.

Leanne was too enchanted with her surroundings to notice where the hostess was taking them. The upper floor was as elegant as the first. From the mezzanine, the sparkling chandelier that hung over the ballroom below was a magnificent display of cut glass twinkling softly.

The hostess motioned for them to follow her through a doorway that led outside to a large balcony surrounded by black wrought-iron lacework. There were several tables covered with cream linen cloths, decorated with fresh flowers of various colors in bud vases that stood next to a small candle centerpiece. Bart held Leanne's chair for her and she sat carefully on the blue velour cushion, hoping not to irritate her sunburn.

"The maître d' will be right with you," the hostess said before leaving them alone.

Leanne looked around her. The roof of the house extended over the balcony, and she imagined that columns of the same style she had seen out front were supporting the floor beneath her.

"Come here," Bart said, rising from his seat to take her hand. They walked to the edge of the balcony, where a courtyard could be seen below them. Flowers and shrubbery bordered a wide, pebbled area with tables. In the center of a large fountain a torch had been lit, casting a rainbow of color into the sprinkling water.

Leanne felt electrified by Bart's touch as he squeezed her hand gently. "Beautiful, isn't it?" he asked.

"Breathtaking," Leanne declared, hypnotized by the movement of the fountain. The whole day had been marvelous. Even the strain at the cove had not been able to ruin their day. Looking into his eyes, Leanne ached to reach up and touch the rugged plane of his cheek.

"Ahem." Leanne looked past Bart to see the maître d' standing with menus in his fidgeting hands. Bart turned and they walked back to the table. "Excuse me," the maître d' said as he stepped forward and handed them the menus. "Wine?"

Bart looked quizzically at Leanne, then shook his head. "Lime fruit water, please." Bart handed the menu back to the man. "And we will start with Shrimp De Jonghe followed by Blanquette de Veau and a side order of frog legs." Bart watched Leanne's face turn pale beneath her sunburn and chuckled. "Would you like to know what you are about to eat?" he asked when they were alone.

"I understood one thing, and that I'm not sure I'm willing to try." She made a face and shivered.

"That must be the frog legs!" Bart laughed. "You'll like them. Trust me." He is so confident, she thought.

"You do trust me, don't you?" Bart asked, the humor gone from his voice as he studied her.

This was it. He was about to ruin the evening by proposing, forcing her to make a decision she wasn't ready to make. She was saved from answering him by the waiter, who brought frosted glasses of sparkling fruit water, setting one in front of her and the other next to Bart's hand that rested on the table. Leanne closed her eyes and breathed deeply. He was holding the white box, that dreadful box.

Bart evidently thought better of presenting her with the gift just yet, for he replaced it in his pocket. Leanne took the green glass stirrer between her fingers and toyed with the slice of lime floating in her glass. "You're quiet this evening," Bart stated matter-of-factly. "Something wrong?"

"I'm just tired, I guess," she answered, hoping he would accept such a simple explanation.

Bart eyed her for a moment, and she was afraid he didn't believe her until, leaning forward, he said, "You got sunburned today, didn't you?" It was more a statement than a question. Leanne was so relieved that he hadn't detected her real feelings that she no longer cared if he knew her skin was blistered. Lowering her dark lashes, she nodded her head hesitantly. "I thought so," he said. "As soon as we get back to the hotel, it will have to be treated." Leanne started to object, but he cocked his head to the side and raised a dark brow. It was a gesture that dared her to defy him.

Pressing her lips together tightly, Leanne turned to see if anyone at the other tables was looking, and as no one was, she bravely declared in controlled tones, "I have been sunburned before, and it hasn't killed me yet!"

"No, and it's not likely to kill you now, but if you don't treat it, you may wish you were dead by morning." Bart sipped his drink and peered at her over the frosty rim of his glass.

She knew he was right. Even now she cringed at every movement. She would never be able to sleep tonight. "I promise to take care of it. Now can we drop the subject?"

Bart twirled the ice around in his glass, staring into it thoughtfully before answering. "As long as you realize that I intend to make sure you keep that promise."

What did he mean? Did he intend to treat her sunburn himself? Mentally, she shook her head. No, she couldn't allow that at all.

"You don't trust me, do you, Leanne?" It was a straightforward question, and she wasn't prepared for it.

"Of course I do. Would I have come all this way from

home with you if I didn't?" Leanne picked up her glass with false calmness, lowering her lashes as she sipped the bubbling liquid, not allowing Bart to see the tears burning behind her eyes. The truth, she was beginning to realize, was that she didn't trust herself any more than she did him.

The waiter interrupted them, placing a large clam-shell stuffed with shrimp on each of their plates. Leanne looked down at her plate, her eyes riveted on the spots of paprika and golden bread crumbs that seasoned the dish. She sampled the appetizer methodically, feeling Bart watching her.

"Good?" he asked, holding his cocktail fork in midair as he waited for her answer.

"Scrumptious," Leanne said, smiling up at him sweetly, glad the subject had been changed. "What is this called again?"

"Shrimp De Jonghe. The shrimp is boiled, then baked in a special De Jonghe butter recipe." Bart pierced a shrimp with his fork and ate the tasty morsel with obvious pleasure.

Leanne smiled. At times he seemed to genuinely enjoy life. "You said you dine here often. But it's so far from Tulsa—"

"You forget that I travel a lot in my profession. We have an offshore rig in the Gulf, and I've had the pleasure of working down here off and on now for several months. I grew up in Louisiana and have an inborn taste for Creole cuisine, and Boudion's serves the best. Agree?" he asked as she took another bite. Leanne had to admit she'd never eaten seafood seasoned quite like this before.

"Do your parents still live in Louisiana?" she asked.

"They're no longer living," Bart said, turning his shrimp over in the sauce absently.

"I'm sorry," Leanne said softly, as she watched him toy with the shrimp. "Tell me about your childhood?" she asked, surprising herself as well as Bart.

"There's not a lot to tell."

"I bet you were a very quiet, shy boy."

Bart laughed, leaning back in his chair and eyeing her thoughtfully. "And you . . . you were a tomboy!"

Leanne blushed. "How did you guess?" She sighed. "You already know so much about me and I know so little about you. Seriously, Bart, I'm interested."

"What do you want to know?"

"What kinds of things did you like to do?" Leanne set her fork down and entwined her fingers under her chin.

"Let's see," Bart began, taking his drink to his lips before continuing. "I liked to fish," he said, a lazy smile crossing his face as he watched Leanne shake her head. "Not good enough, huh? Well, I was a Cub Scout," he ventured, then added, bragging, "I received all the badges and awards available and even got a trophy in marksmanship."

"Then you've always been successful," Leanne speculated with admiration.

"I wouldn't call myself successful," he said quietly. "Oh, I admit I've achieved a lot in my lifetime. Some of it good and some bad." Bart took Leanne's hand and held it between both of his. "Taking you out has been an achievement I'm quite proud of."

Leanne withdrew her hand. "I see!" she exclaimed,

pretending to be indignant. "You must admit, I gave you a run for your money!" she added with a laugh.

"I get the feeling sometimes that you're still running," Bart said seriously.

The waiter brought the rest of their meal, and Leanne welcomed the interruption. She surprised herself and Bart by bravely eating the frog legs, which resembled skinny chicken legs and tasted as such. Bart shared his experiences growing up with his father's shrimping business and Leanne was pleased that Bart was beginning to open up to her.

Instead of going back to the hotel when they left Boudion's, they took a taxi to the ferry landing. The warm sea breeze caressed her face as Leanne stood next to Bart by the rail of the boat. There were few cars on the ferry, and she felt that the trip was being made across the channel for her and Bart alone. The stars were bright and the moon still reflected the orange fire of the sun. The sound of a foghorn could be heard in the distance as it pierced the stillness of the night.

Leanne glanced at Bart. His elbows rested on the rail and his fingers locked as his arms extended in front of him. He was staring into the dark water, engrossed in his thoughts, seemingly unaware that she was even there. Leanne turned toward him, her side against the boat, her hands folded as they lay on the rail. "Penny for your thoughts," she said, daring to hope he would confide them.

Bart chuckled. "Are you sure you want to know?" he asked, still looking into the water.

"I'm sure."

"I was just thinking about the gift I've been carrying

around all evening." Slowly he turned his head to see her expression, but she quickly glanced away, not wanting to meet his eyes. "Mind telling me what's wrong with my giving you a present?"

Leanne swallowed. The air was salty and the tear that had escaped was bitter. What could she say— "I'm not ready to make a commitment"—when he hadn't even asked her to make one yet? "It isn't you, Bart, or your gift. It's me. I'm just not sure I . . ." Leanne tried to find the words to explain her fear, but the words just didn't come.

The ferry landed and the cars drove past them, exiting the boat. As there were no cars waiting to return to the island, the ferry began its trip back. The silence that had accompanied them during their ride over began to ring in her ears, as Leanne knew Bart was waiting for her to finish her sentence. Finally he returned his gaze to the water, which rippled softly in the moonlight, now a frosty glow as it hung among the stars.

"It may not be at all what you think it is," Bart said, breaking the deafening silence. "You don't have to be so afraid of me, Leanne. I wouldn't hurt you." He turned again toward her, this time taking each of her arms in his powerful but gentle hands, his thumbs moving slowly against the soft material of her sleeves, making chaos of her already confused emotions. Leanne let her eyes meet his, wanting so much to believe him.

A large hand came up to brush away a tear trailing down her cheek. Leaning forward, Bart touched her forehead with his full lips and drew her into his arms, holding her head against his chest, where she broke into uncontrollable sobs.

"I'm sorry, Bart," she managed to say after a while. "I can't help myself. Eric . . ."

"But I'm not Eric. Why can't you get that through that pretty head of yours?" His voice was soft as his warm breath moved close to her face, his lips brushing hers.

Leanne felt torn. Half of her wanted to cast caution to the wind and return Bart's kiss, while the other half still worried what fate the opening of the little white box would bring her. In a moment of recklessness her fingers grasped the lapels of his jacket and, standing on tiptoe, Leanne moved closer, answering his plea with her own. When their lips parted, Leanne rested her head on his chest and he hugged her against him while he reached in his jacket for the box.

"As much as I'd like it to be, it isn't what you think," Bart said as he led her to a bench and sat her down next to him. Lifting the small package in his hand, he began to rip the glossy paper from around the box. A blue velvet container appeared, and as he opened it Leanne gasped at the beauty of its contents.

A tiny, clear figure shaped from the hand-blown glass into an angel with gold wings lay against the blue satin of the interior, its golden halo looped around a fine, gold chain. Leanne watched his large hand remove the pendant from the box and fumble with the clasp. Holding it in front of her, Bart smiled.

"You see, you did all that worrying for nothing." Leaning forward, he placed the chain around her neck, his face close to hers as he fastened it. She held her hair off her neck, and when he had finished with the necklace, she moved her hands over his shoulders and kissed his rough cheek.

"It's beautiful, Bart. Thank you," she whispered.

The ferry docked and they walked arm in arm back to their waiting cab.

When they entered the hotel, Bart asked the desk to send a bellman up with aloe vera cream from the drugstore. Leanne was about to protest again, but once more Bart arched a daring brow.

"Thought I'd forget, didn't you?" he asked when they got into the elevator.

"No, I . . . well, yes, I hoped that you would have left it up to me. I had said I would take care of it."

"With what?" he asked as the elevator opened on their floor. Stepping out behind Leanne, Bart took her key from his pocket and added with a wink as he unlatched the door, "Were you going to use cold cream or toothpaste?"

"Bart Hall, you're . . ."

"Hopeless again?"

"No! Impossible!" she said, a pouty look on her face.

"You'll be glad I am by morning." Bart pushed open the door and moved across the hall to open his own. Leanne followed him, stopping in the doorway to watch as he tossed his hanging bag onto the bed and unzipped it. He pulled out the navy blue polo shirt he had worn that morning when he picked her up. "First thing to do is get you into something more comfortable." He flung the shirt toward her, smiling at the bewildered look on her face as she caught the shirt. Leanne allowed him to propel her back to her room where he bent to kiss the top of her head. "Remember, you promised," he said, running a strong finger down the bridge of her nose.

"I'm not a child, Bart," she said, pushing his hand away. "And all that I promised was that I would take care of it!"

"I'm just being helpful." Bart picked the shirt up off the floor at her feet where she had dropped it, handing it to her before leaving the room, closing the door behind him.

"Ooh!" Leanne exclaimed, throwing the shirt at the door, watching with fury as it slid noiselessly to the floor. "What an arrogant . . . bully he is!" she said aloud, her hands planted firmly on her hips. "I won't wear it!" she screamed louder, to enable him to hear her through the door. He made no response, and Leanne suddenly found herself laughing. How utterly ridiculous this whole mess was! One minute she melted in his arms, and the next she was screaming at him. For a fleeting moment she wondered what it would be like to be married to him, to see him day and night, to be in his arms always. Leanne walked over to the door and picked up the shirt, holding it to her as if she were holding him.

Though he had only worn the shirt for the few hours it had taken to fly to Galveston, it bore the distinct smell of musk and tobacco that she had grown to love. Leanne untied the ribbon of her dress and slipped it over her head, aware once more of the burning sensation she had forgotten. Slowly she pulled the soft shirt on, then took off her slip and stockings, replacing them with the jeans she had worn that morning. Her cotton blouse might have been as soft as his shirt, but she was glad he hadn't thought of it. She felt close to him, wearing his clothes. Leanne folded the print blouse and laid it back in the suitcase along with her dress.

She moved to the full-length mirror. The shirt hung halfway to her knees and fell off her shoulders by at least two inches. He really is a big man, she thought, laughing to herself as she tucked most of the shirt into her jeans. Leanne brushed her hair into a ponytail, then pulled on her tennis shoes. She felt like the child she had told Bart she wasn't, but it was a good, carefree feeling.

A knock sounded at the door. "The bellman brought the cream," Bart was saying as she opened the door. A smile curved his lips and his eyes twinkled as he took in her appearance.

"Now that's what I love about you—versatility."

Leanne blushed, not sure if she should be mad or not. "And it is your silver tongue that makes you so devastating," she retorted. The word love had made her heart race for a moment, but she realized he was only kidding with her. He laughed softly as he moved into the room, the tube of cream in his hand. "Thank you for bringing the cream. Now you can give it to me and leave."

She stood with one hand extended and the other on her hip, waiting in mock impatience.

Bart tossed the tube into the air, catching it and tossing it again, then watching it land on the bed. "Pretty bossy little thing, aren't you?" He moved closer and grabbed her extended hand before she could withdraw it. Putting it to his lips, he touched it lightly; then, still holding it, he reached across the bed for the cream with his free hand. "As you wish." He placed the tube in her hand, closing her fingers around it with his. "If you need any help . . . ?"

"I'll do fine, thank you," Leanne said, watching him

as he walked out of the room, turning to smile mischievously before closing the door behind him.

Awkwardly she managed to smooth the cream across her shoulders and back, then packed the tube in her suitcase. It was getting late and she knew they would soon be leaving for the airport. It had been a wonderful day, but now it was over.

Chapter Seven

It was sprinkling when the cab pulled into Stewart Field. A suitable ending to a beautiful day, Leanne thought, watching the windshield wipers swish back and forth. She felt a touch of sadness that it was all over. Bart was next to her, his arm across her shoulders even though they were lost in his shirt. She'd felt ridiculous when they had left the hotel; though Bart assured her she looked fine, she knew she didn't. At least they would be in his private plane and she wouldn't have to see anyone else since it would be late when they reached Tulsa.

"Wait in the cab while I load the suitcases and do a preflight inspection," Bart said when the cab stopped near the hangar.

Leanne watched as he and the driver carried their bags across the parking lot to the small plane. After he had loaded them, he went inside the control building.

The small airport was practically deserted. Bart had said it used to be pretty busy, but now only small private planes used it. The darkness was pierced only by small blue lights that marked the runway and the golden glow of a light from a distant farmhouse.

The cab door opened and Bart climbed in next to her. "Are we ready?" she asked, wondering why he had gotten back into the cab.

"I don't think so. They say the weather is going to get worse, and I thought maybe we should stay."

"Are you sure?" Leanne was uneasy about staying the night with Bart so close. "It's only eleven now; we could probably be home by one."

Bart read the fear on Leanne's face and sighed as he leaned back in the seat. "We could try," he said, staring at the vinyl ceiling of the cab. He turned toward her and smiled. "What does Eric look like?"

"Eric?" Leanne was puzzled. "Why on earth would you ask me that now?"

"I was just curious whether we bore a resemblance or something." Bart's eyes narrowed and he leaned across her, his face close to hers. "Give me a chance, will you?" he whispered, his hazel eyes piercing hers. Still, Leanne couldn't give him the encouragement he wanted. He sat back and looked out the window at the pouring rain. Then, taking her hand, he opened the door. "Come on, let's go."

They ran toward the Cessna and clambered across the metal wing to the cabin, still warm from sitting all day in the hot sun. Bart started the engines, and soon they were heading down the runway, the blue lights turning into a blue streak as they traveled faster.

Leanne felt herself being held against the back of her seat as Bart pushed the throttles forward and the plane began to rise.

The cabin had reached a comfortable temperature by now and Leanne relaxed, feeling sure they would be in Tulsa within a few hours. The rain had cleared and she could see the stars above her, so close she felt she could touch them. How could the weather get worse when the sky was so beautiful? Leanne looked toward Bart. He hadn't turned the autopilot on as he had on their flight down, and he was concentrating on the instrument panel in front of him as though he expected it to change suddenly. Leanne examined the panel, but she could see nothing unusual about the way the needle idled. Maybe he was angry with her for wanting to return tonight. She leaned back in her seat and rested her head against the window, sleepily gazing at the mesmerizing city lights below her. . . .

Leanne sat up with a jolt. She must have fallen asleep. Wiping her drowsy eyes with the back of her hand, she tried to determine what had awakened her. The loud, crashing sound came again, and she jumped.

"It's thunder," Bart explained, glancing only momentarily in her direction before returning his concentration to the panel. "We're going to have to make an emergency landing at Tulsa International."

Leanne tensed as she tried to see the lights from the ground again, but neither they nor the stars were visible. A quick flash of light blinded her and she nearly screamed. Blinking her eyes, she looked at Bart. He was still concentrating on the panel and the blackness before them. Not wanting to disturb him, Leanne sat quietly, praying for God to be with Bart and get them home safely.

"We're going to have a rough landing," Bart said, not taking his eyes off the panel. "I can't see a thing. I've radioed ahead and asked for a radar vector to lead us in."

"What do you mean, you can't see? What do you need to see? Aren't the instruments enough?"

"Yes, but it's risky business relying solely on a compass and needles in a plane this size. Without visual contact, you're flying blind. I'd just rather not chance it."

A sheet of water blanketed the windshield, and sudden fear gripped Leanne. Her only thought was that she could die and never know how Bart really felt about her, nor would he know how much he meant to her. She looked again at his face, on which the strain of concentration still showed. He glanced at her and she forced a brave smile. Now wasn't the time for a last will and testament. He had enough on his mind without worrying about her. Dear God, she prayed silently, give me faith.

Lightning danced about them, and Leanne could make out the wing of the plane stretching into the storm like a huge arm that held them up. A gentle peace entered her being and she knew God was with them. Walls of blackness surrounded them again, and as her eyes refocused she could make out a haze of golden light directly in front of the plane. A voice came over the radio, and Bart responded. Leanne had no idea what was being said. She was so relieved to see the ground again and know she was to live through the terrible ordeal.

Bart lowered the landing gear and soon they touched down, easily gliding down the runway. Leanne's eyes followed the white line that marked the center, and when the plane slowed, she turned to face Bart. He was smiling at her with an I-told-you-so look in his eyes. He had been right, she thought. They could have been killed, and all because of her foolish mistrust.

Bart parked the plane as close to the buildings as possible, for there were several other private planes in the area that had most likely been grounded. Leanne helped him get their bags from the rear of the plane and they ran through the torrential rain toward the airport entrance. The lobby was packed with people waiting either for the departure of a delayed flight or for the arrival of loved ones.

Leanne followed Bart to the operations office and waited by the door, suitcases at her feet, while he talked to the man behind the counter. The airport was cold and she began to shiver. She was soaking wet and Bart's shirt clung to her like a second skin. Her hair, still in the ponytail, had loosened and, feeling self-conscious, she tried to replace the wet strands. Bart finished at the counter and came over to Leanne, who was looking like a lost orphan. He smiled at her pitifully and dug into his suitcase for a jacket, placing it gently around her drooping shoulders.

"I'll have you home soon and you can get into some dry clothes." He looked at her, evidently concerned. "Are you all right?"

"I'm fine." She glanced up at him and knew he didn't

believe her. "Really," she assured him, grabbing her suitcase and overnight bag. "But can we please get out of here?" she pleaded, looking around her at the people who were staring at them.

Bart laughed. "Of course," he said, taking the suitcase from her. "There should be a taxi right out this door."

But there wasn't. Instead, there were crowds of people waiting to hail the first cab to return. Going back into the lobby, Bart directed Leanne to a chair near the public phones. "Wait here, angel, and I'll find something." Leanne sat on the cold vinyl chair, sinking into the soft cushion and wishing she could go to sleep right there.

She could hear Bart's voice as he made several calls. She knew he was getting a negative reply with each dial of the phone. He was trying so hard. Leaving their bags near the chair, she joined Bart in the long paneled room lined with pay phones. He smiled reassuringly when he saw her, but when the party answered his questions, his smile faded.

"I'm sorry, Leanne," he said, hanging up the receiver. "I have no one else to call. That is, except for Rob," he added hesitantly.

Leanne noticed the tiredness in his voice. He was soaked as much as she, and his black hair glistened in the light as drops of rain still beaded the thick strands. The wine and gray stripes of his shirt were darker and the white background was spotted as parts of it clung to his chest. She knew his hesitation to call her father was a matter of pride.

"Dad won't mind, really," she assured him.

"I know," Bart said, a half grin on his face as he began to dial her father's number.

A small group of people had gathered at a pay phone near them and Leanne felt conspicuously grubby in comparison. Yet, despite the storm, Bart still managed to look good. She examined his profile, noting his strong features, the slant of his nose, the deep dimple in his cheek, the jut of his proud chin. He spoke momentarily into the receiver, then replaced it.

"Want some coffee while we wait?" he asked.

Leanne placed her hand in the fold of his arm, smiling into his hazel eyes. "Sounds wonderful."

Bart squeezed her fingers reassuringly as they passed the well-dressed group, making her feel beautiful despite the disarray of her appearance. She watched him help load their bags on a cart. His hands were strong and capable, yet she knew how gentle they could be, how they could make her tremble with just his touch upon her hair. Bart paid the porter to watch their luggage, and they headed for the coffee shop.

"I don't think you're going to be able to go to Washington in the morning now," Rob Masterson said to Bart as they loaded their luggage in the trunk of the car. "The weatherman says it will rain hard all day. Of course that wouldn't matter to you after flying around in this mess," he added, unlocking the passenger door before moving to the driver's side and climbing in. "Sharon's been sick with worry," he continued as he started the engine.

Seated between them with Bart's arm across her shoulders, Leanne listened to her father carry on. She felt like a teenager coming home late from her first date. Sighing, she glanced at Bart. He smiled at her and winked. Returning his smile, Leanne relaxed, and together they humored her outspoken father.

By the time they reached the edge of town the rain was pelting the car from all sides. "No need to go clear out to the other air strip for your truck tonight, Bart," Rob said, as another sheet of water hit the windshield. "We've got plenty of room at the house to keep us all comfortable."

"Looks as though I don't have a choice," Bart said, hugging Leanne against his side. "Do you think you could run me out to get my truck in the morning?" he asked her quietly, his breath stirring the soft ringlets of hair near her ear. Leanne shivered and Bart kissed her temple. "Well?" he whispered.

"I'd be glad to," she said, turning to look into his smiling eyes.

"Are there wedding bells in the distance?" She heard her father say.

"Dad!" Leanne exclaimed, facing him.

"Just kidding, princess," he said, patting her knee. "You know, your mother and I thought you two went to Galveston to elope, until I talked to Bart this afternoon."

Leanne felt the blood rush to her face. "Really, Dad!" was all she could say. She felt Bart's eyes on her during the rest of the trip, but she avoided looking at him until they'd arrived at her parents' home.

"I'm going to let Leanne show you the guest room," her father said as he set her suitcase on the floor of the living room. "I'm beat." Rob Masterson kissed his daughter's forehead and smiled at Bart. "Good night you two. Don't stay up all night," he added as he sauntered out of the room.

Bart dropped his bag on the sofa and carried Leanne's to the nearest bedroom. "This room yours?" he asked, arching a brow, then proceeding to flip on the light after Leanne nodded her head.

"Why didn't you tell me it was my dad that called?" she asked, leaning against the doorframe.

"It was business," Bart explained. "I didn't think about it."

"He was checking up on me," she declared. "I can't believe he would do such a thing."

"Leanne," Bart said, taking her arms in his hands, "I said it was business."

"I'm going to have a talk with him tomorrow."

"I don't think you should."

"He's my father and I'm not going to argue with you about it," Leanne said defiantly, standing her ground.

Bart stepped back and eyed her from head to toe. She looked like a spoiled child throwing a tantrum. His shirt swallowed her small frame and the band that held her ponytail had loosened, so the nearly dry strands of loose hair were falling in ringlets about her face.

"You don't look nearly as tough as you sound," Bart said, a hand resting on the wall beside her head. Suddenly, she didn't feel so tough, either. The fresh smell of rain lingered in the air, filling her nostrils as she breathed deeply.

"Well, you'd better not try me," she warned, managing to sound more in control than she was.

"Maybe I should," he dared, brushing her cheek softly with his lips, his free hand pivoting her chin slightly so he could touch the other side of her face.

"Bart . . ." Leanne began, but his thumb gently moved across her lips, hushing her. His eyes held hers as he reached into her hair to free it of the band. The heavy folds of brown silky hair fell to her shoulders and down her back.

"I'm still going to have that talk." Leanne spoke softly, not as sure of herself as she had been before, her hands clutching the doorframe behind her.

Bart lifted her hair in his hands, rubbing it between his fingers the way one would a fine cloth. "I love your hair," he said, his eyes roaming her face and the silken waves that framed it. Suddenly he dropped his hands, slipping them into his trouser pockets. "Your father loves you, Leanne, and he was concerned."

Stunned, Leanne stood cemented to the spot. So her father had been checking up on her, and now Bart was covering for him. She felt his hands on her arms, gently pulling her out of the doorway so he could pass through. All of a sudden, she was furious. Slamming the door behind him, Leanne stomped to the adjoining bathroom, not caring whether she woke her parents. The hot water of the shower matched her temper, but by the time she went to bed she was too exhausted to care anymore.

Leanne awoke sometime during the night, sneezing. Disoriented, she reached for the bedside lamp, fumbling with the fixture until a pale light flooded the room. Sneezing again, she wrapped her grandfather's old Indian robe around her shoulders and tiptoed down the hall. Crossing the den to the kitchen, she flipped on the light switch.

"What time is it?" Bart asked, startling her.

Quickly, Leanne turned to find him relaxed in her father's recliner. "I don't know."

"My watch is in my jacket. Will you get it?" he said, stretching as he moved to sit up.

Leanne looked around the room for his jacket and found it folded across a chair. Reaching in the pocket, she brought out the watch and moved hesitantly back into the lighted kitchen.

"It's nearly four," she said.

"You didn't get much sleep. What woke you?"

Suddenly she sneezed. "Is that enough of an answer?" she asked, rubbing her nose with a tissue. "And why are you up?"

"Couldn't sleep."

"Should I make you some coffee?" she asked.

"Only if you're going to join me." Bart stood and followed her into the kitchen. She sneezed again. "You need a cup of hot tea," he said, obviously concerned.

Leanne ignored him and made a pot of coffee while Bart watched her from the small kitchen table.

"You're so domestic indoors, and so crafty outside. It's amazing that you're still single," he finally said, breaking the silence and reminding her of her father's comment the night before.

"Oh really?" she teased, trying to make light of the conversation. "Because I look so homey in my natural state?"

"Actually, there's a lot of beauty being wasted. Some lucky man should wake up to your sleepy Irish eyes and mussed curls." Bart's gaze was so intense that she quickly turned away.

"I'm not sure I'm ready for marriage," she said,

laughing carelessly. But her heart raced when she placed the cups on the table and sat across from him. She watched as he lifted his cup, his tanned arms appearing even darker against the white sleeves of the cotton shirt he wore. His eyes seemed to probe at her over the rim of his cup as he brought it to his full lips.

"What time do you need to leave?" Leanne asked, trying to change the subject.

"After you tell me just what this Eric character did to make you so skittish." Bart returned his cup to its saucer, watching her face, intending to read her thoughts.

Leanne laughed nervously. "Is that what you're losing sleep over?"

"You might say that."

Leanne sat back, her fingers playing with the links of his watchband on her wrist. "I've already told you. I was just young and, I thought, in love. I thought he loved me, too. I believed in him and was miserable every time he went on his *business* trips to New York. It was after he had left on one of those trips that I discovered he had been engaged to someone else and had married her several months before. I was devastated. I felt used, and if he had had his way, I would have been. As it was, he had me dependent on him for my happiness."

"And ever since, you've been out to prove to the world that Leanne Masterson can make it on her own, that she doesn't need anyone."

Leanne looked up at his sympathetic smile. "I don't need your pity, Bart!" Leanne stood up and stalked toward the window. She knew he was just trying to be understanding, but she didn't want his pity. She had dealt herself too much of it in the past to accept anyone else's. It was all over now, and she wanted to leave all memories of that unpleasant time buried with the past.

"You aren't the only one who has lived with misery and pain, you know," Bart said, his voice low.

Leanne turned to face him. He held the delicate coffee cup in his powerful hand as he watched her expression change from defiance to puzzlement. "I know that," she said, walking back to her chair. "You, I'm sure, have had your share. Everyone, I suppose, has had to deal with unhappiness at one time or another. I don't mean to say they haven't."

"It's just that when it's yours, it's harder to look at it so objectively." He finished her thought for her, though she hadn't been sure what words to use to express herself.

"And who are you angry with, Bart?" she asked, sure he was speaking from his own experience.

"Myself," he answered, nonchalantly filling his cup with coffee again.

"Why should you be angry with yourself? You've done a wonderful job raising your sons. You've obviously been successful in your profession, and you've traveled the world, to boot."

"I told you that my traveling has taken me away from Matt and Charlie and that it is their grandmother who has done such a wonderful job raising them, not me."

"But, Bart, you're making it up to them. They'll be thrilled to find you've had the construction for the cabin started while they've been gone. The three of you are so close. And they love you very much."

"Now look who's handing out pity." Bart chuckled. "It isn't their love I'm worried about. I know they love me, just as I know they feel my love for them." It was Bart's turn to stand, his pent-up emotions taking control of his energy and not allowing him to sit still. "No, it's their forgiveness I worry about," he said, walking to the window as she had done. "Someday they will find out that I wasn't there when Carol died; that I was off on the other side of the world when she needed me." Bart faced Leanne, and the frown on her brow told him she didn't understand. "I know I told you that I didn't start traveling until after she died, but this was, I thought, a once-in-a-lifetime deal. A chance to make the money we needed for a specialist—another specialist, that is."

Leanne fought the pity that she felt for him. She knew he didn't want it, and she didn't really want to give it to him. Instead, he needed understanding, maybe a few words of encouragement. "How long was she sick, Bart?" she asked, trying to make her voice strong.

"It seemed like years, but actually it was only fifteen months." Bart sat back down on the sofa. "She spent the last two of those in the hospital." He stared into the full cup of coffee still sitting where he had left it. "Coffee's cold," he said, looking up at Leanne. "I don't really want to talk about it anymore," he added before she could say the words forming on her lips.

"It isn't the boys who need to forgive you, is it, Bart? It's yourself. You can't forgive yourself for not being there."

"I said I didn't want to talk about it," Bart insisted as he crossed the room and emptied the rest of his coffee into the sink. When he came back to the table, Leanne stood, taking the cup from him and placing it next to hers. Holding his large hand in her small palm, she searched his eyes; years of pain seemed to fill their depths. "It isn't your fault, Bart. I know you've been told that before, and you didn't believe it. You have searched all over the world for the peace that only God can give you. Only He can help you to overcome the anger you feel for yourself."

"God? I have no reason to turn to God!" Bart said, pulling away from her and pacing the floor like a caged lion. All too late, Leanne regretted having touched on such a painful subject.

"But, Bart," she insisted, "God can—"

"Forget God! Where was He when Charlie woke up in the night crying for his mother, or when Mathew needed her arms to cuddle him? And what about *my* arms, Leanne? What about the wife I needed?"

"It's normal to feel angry and alone, Bart. In fact, most people I know who have gone through such a tragedy seem to have problems with bitterness. We all want to blame someone or something, but we can't blame God, Bart. He sees so much more than we do. Trusting Him with your future is a vital part of your faith."

Bart put his back to her and faced the window, watching the treeline sway against the moonlit sky. "And what about you, Leanne?" he asked without turning around. "What about this great faith you claim to have? Are you trusting God when you cringe in your corner, afraid to love again?" Slowly he turned to face her, his eyes mirroring her thoughts before she averted her gaze to the gold watch she still wore. Thrusting it into his palm, she glared at him, angry that he would use her words against her. But his fingers closed around hers. "Are you?" he asked again, his voice softer as he searched her face and realized the impact his question had on her.

"I . . . don't know," Leanne answered, pulling her hand away. "I never thought about it that way."

"Perhaps you should," Bart said gently.

"Are you saying I don't practice what I preach?" she asked, the hurt in her voice evident.

Bart placed a strong finger under her chin, turning her to face him. "I'm saying that you are a beautiful woman and you can't hide yourself away forever. If you'd listen, I'm sure God Himself has been trying to tell you that."

"You don't fight fair," Leanne whispered.

"Is that what we're doing?" Bart asked innocently. "In that case, let's kiss and make up." Slowly, he cupped her face in his hands and drew her into a kiss. "That's enough fighting for tonight," he said, ushering Leanne toward the hall. "Try to get a few more hours of sleep."

"Only if you promise to think about what we've discussed," Leanne insisted.

"You drive a hard bargain," Bart teased. "But how can I refuse when you ask so sweetly?"

Chapter Eight

Leanne adjusted the rearview mirror so that she could see her own reflection. Three days had passed since that night at her parents' house, and now she had to face them, knowing they would question her about her trip to Galveston. Her eyes were bright with anticipation. Did they really think she would have eloped with Bart? She picked up the souvenirs from the seat next to her and opened the car door. Her mother would have died if she had, she thought, walking up the sidewalk to her parents' home. And Dad . . . well, there was no telling how he would react.

"I heard your car," Sharon Masterson said as she opened the door before Leanne reached it. "I thought you would be walking over, and I couldn't imagine who else would be coming out so early."

"I have to go into town after breakfast. Bart asked

me to pick the boys up for him. He won't be at the apartment when they come home from camp, and their grandmother is ill."

"I hope it's nothing serious," her mother said, stepping aside and letting Leanne pass.

"I don't think it is," she replied, heading for the kitchen, her mother close behind her. "Anyway, Bart has decided to hire a housekeeper to watch over the boys, but since he hasn't found one yet, I volunteered to help out while I'm on vacation."

"Are you still going to be able to pick Rhonda up from the airport in the morning?" her mother asked.

Leanne had been walking sideways, half facing her mother and half facing the direction she was walking. "Wild horses couldn't keep me away from that airport tomorrow!" she said with a laugh. Turning around, she saw her father at the breakfast table. "Morning, Dad."

"Good morning, princess," he said, putting down his newspaper to grin at his daughter. "I'll bet you're glad your vacation time coincided with Rhonda's trip."

"You're right," she said, pouring a cup of coffee. "I haven't seen her since she graduated from law school." Since Leanne and Rhonda had grown up together, Rhonda was the closest thing to a sister Leanne had.

"I hope you don't let her talk you into any of her harebrained schemes, the way she used to," he said with a chuckle.

"We were pretty brainy, weren't we?" Leanne teased as she leaned against the counter. "I only wish I had more of my vacation time left."

"Just how is this vacation of yours coming along?" Rob Masterson asked. "Guess your new beau's keeping you busy."

Leanne sat in the chair next to him. "Now, Dad, you know you're my favorite beau." Leanne winked up at her mother and watched her shake her head.

"You spoil that man rotten, Leanne, and then I'm the one who has to put up with him when you leave." Sharon Masterson poured more coffee into their cups and joined them at the small table, a smile across her face.

"Now this guy has you baby-sitting," her father continued, ignoring his wife's remarks.

"Make up your mind, Rob. You're the one who introduced her to Bart."

"Sure I did, and he's a good man, too. Don't get me wrong; it isn't Bart I object to at all. I just want to know when *she's* going to start keeping his house and giving me a grandson so *I* can baby-sit."

"Dad, you're crazy, you know that?" Leanne laughed.

"Well, if you latch on to Bart, then I can have a head start on learning this grandparent business."

"Leanne, do you want to help me with breakfast and let the old man get back to reading his paper before he starts calling me granny?" Leanne's mother asked as she left the table.

"Sure, Mom." Leanne joined in her laughter and stood, bending over her father's shoulder. "If it will make you feel better, Dad, I'm glad you introduced me to Bart and I'm sure he wouldn't mind if you played grandpa to his children. They don't have one living, you know."

Rob Masterson took his daughter's hand that rested on his shoulder and squeezed it. "You know I'm only kidding with you, princess." He turned to face her, a serious look in his blue eyes. "You just take your time. Don't let a silly old man's teasing rush you into something you'll be sorry for. Bart's a good man, all right, but I'm not sure he's good enough for you."

Leanne placed a kiss on his soft cheek. "Dad, I don't think I'll ever find anyone who will meet your standards, but if anyone would, Bart would."

"I'm glad to hear you say that. Gives me a little hope." He laughed and swatted at her leg. "Now go help your mother get some grub on the table. I'm starved."

Excitedly, Leanne drove into Tulsa. It would be easy to find Bart's apartment. She didn't know it until yesterday, but she had been passing it on her way to work all this time. Her father was anxious to play grandpa with Mathew and Charlie, but he would have never guessed how good she felt this morning knowing she had the full day ahead to play at being their mother. It was a foolish idea, she knew, but she had been obsessed with the thought all morning. "Who knows," she said aloud, "he may ask me." Marriage was on her mind. Hadn't Bart said that he wished the pendant had been something else, implying the ring she had dreaded? Oddly enough, her feelings were beginning to change. Her thoughts drifted as she hummed to the tune on the car radio.

Leanne pulled into the drive that led to Bart's apartment house and, parking near the entrance, dug into her purse for the passkey Bart had given her. The doorman acknowledged her with a nod of his head when she entered the building and headed for the elevators situated in a corner of the large lobby. Impatiently, she waited for the elevator to stop on Bart's floor, and when it finally did, she made her way happily down the corridor in search of the right number. At last she stood in front of the door to Bart's apartment. Hesitantly, she inserted the key.

As the lock clicked, Leanne opened the door to a room filled with Bart's presence. His rugged nature was revealed in the heavy, dark wood furniture covered with thick leather cushions. A matching console lined one long wall, creating a collage of leather-bound books amid a collection of miniature ships accented by shiny brass objects scattered here and there. Above the fireplace hung an old-world map made three-dimensional by the small wooden globe on the mantel. Leanne dropped her purse onto a captain-style bar-stool and moved to the patio door revealed through soft beige curtains. A large balcony overlooked Tulsa, making her appreciate the city as she had never done before.

Leanne glanced at her watch: nine-thirty. Mathew and Charlie weren't due until ten. The aroma of coffee was still in the air, and Leanne wished she had come earlier to have coffee with Bart before he left. She hadn't seen him or talked to him since their first night back from Galveston.

She ventured farther down a paneled hallway, needing to see more of his personality as revealed in his home. An open door led into a bedroom decorated with model planes hanging from the ceiling and sturdy bunk beds set up in an L shape, with a desk and shelves under one end of the upper bunk. Probably Charlie's,

Leanne thought with a smile. Matching shelves held a stereo and television set on one wall, and the scattered toys in a corner were obviously Mathew's. The whole apartment intrigued her: it was as if she were looking into the personal lives of the people she had grown to love.

As she ventured still farther Leanne found Bart's study and knew she was nearing his bedroom when the musky smell of his after-shave filled the air. Excitement overwhelmed her as she entered the room. However, it was soon replaced by a sickening sensation in the pit of her stomach. Atop the rumpled king-size bed a soft peach robe lay next to an open overnight case filled with makeup and female toiletries. The strong smell of coffee suddenly wafted into the room, causing Leanne to whirl around and come face to face with the owner of the night case.

"Hi, I'm Laura, and you must be Leanne," the tall blond woman in a sheer negligee said, before sipping her coffee. "I've been trying to call you all morning."

"I haven't been home." Leanne touched a cool hand to her flushed face. The room had suddenly grown uncomfortably warm.

"I wanted to tell you that I could keep the boys today," the blonde said, moving back down the hall, leaving Leanne to follow. "I decided to stay in town a while longer and there was no need to bother you with keeping the kids." The woman kept walking, her narrow hips swaying beneath the flimsy material of her gown as she moved. "I haven't seen Matt or Charlie in a long time and, well, I feel as if they are practically mine since . . ."

Leanne's heart raced. She had just been able to trust Bart. She had let all her defenses down. She could hear the woman chattering to her from the kitchen area, but Leanne had stopped listening, stopped walking. Tears burned behind her eyes. Hurriedly she reached for her purse, wanting to leave before the woman came back into the room and before the tears fell, humiliating her even more.

She jerked the front door open and hurried past the elevators, not wanting to chance running into the boys on their way up. Her heart ached as it pounded heavily in her chest, making it difficult to breathe as she ran down the three flights of stairs, tears blurring her vision.

When she reached the privacy of her car, she clutched the steering wheel and cried until her head throbbed. *How could he?* she kept asking herself over and over. How could he think she would be such a fool as to allow him to . . . She had been a fool, a fool ever to have allowed him to enter her heart and win her trust . . . the precious trust she had guarded for so long, the trust that he'd shattered along with her heart and her dreams.

Leanne drove for miles, not caring where she was going as long as it took her away from familiar surroundings that would be sure to stir her memories. She didn't dare go home to face the solitude waiting for her there as it always had and probably always would.

It was nearly dark when Leanne turned down the highway that would take her home. Home . . . she wished she could go anywhere else *but* home. But there was no other place to go. She still had a week left of her vacation, and she didn't want to spend it with her parents. In fact, she decided not to tell her parents anything about her trouble with Bart. She couldn't face her mother's sad eyes and her father's matchmaking again.

Pulling into the driveway, she cut the engine off and sat in the dark, staring out across the creek, remembering the first day she had met Bart. The cabin he was having erected could be seen through the trees, and she wondered how she would live here constantly confronted with his coming and going . . . hearing his voice as he called to Mathew and Charlie, seeing them all fishing on the creek bank that she was forced to share. Leanne closed her eyes to the pain that once more began to tear at her heartstrings. "Mathew and Charlie"—she whispered their names. She loved them, too. Now what would she tell them? How would she explain that she couldn't see them again . . . that she couldn't bear to see the resemblance Charlie had to his father or hear Mathew's shy voice asking when he would see her again? Leanne bit her lower lip, willing the tears not to fall, but again they streaked her face.

After drying her eyes, she braced herself to face the evening alone. She knew how it would be. The lonely emptiness would swallow her, choking her in her own self-pity. Slowly she walked up the redwood steps to the deck. She hated self-pity. She had to get a hold on herself, she thought. Taking a deep breath, she faced the door. It wasn't that she didn't like being alone; she lived alone. But there was a difference between being alone and being lonely, and tonight she felt desperately lonely. She could go to Stephen, but she had to stop turning to him for comfort. Someday he would have someone of his own. There was always the pastor, she thought as she unlocked the door. But she knew what he would say. He would sympathetically tell her to pray about it, that God would help her through the crisis.

Leanne went inside and slammed the door behind her, angry with the world. Of course God would see her through her crisis if she could stop feeling sorry for herself long enough to pray. But depression was already taking over; it was too late for reasoning. She didn't care anymore. She drifted to the sofa in a daze, knowing the right thing to do but unable to do it.

The telephone rang, but she let it ring on while she stared at the instrument, a blank look on her face. Soon it stopped and she moved to the kitchen, where she put on the teakettle. The shrill ring of the phone pierced the room again. Ignoring it, she set a coffee mug and the instant coffee on the table. Again and again the sound filled the room. Leanne closed her eyes and banged the teaspoon full of coffee crystals on the table, scattering the little brown rocks everywhere. Why did he persist? she wondered. She knew it had to be Bart. They had made plans to go out for dinner with the boys when he returned from his business trip this evening.

Finally, the silence she prayed for came, only to echo painfully in her ears. She cleaned up the crystals and made herself a cup of coffee, settling in front of the bay window, becoming lost in her thoughts again.

She was bringing the steaming liquid to her lips when the shrill of the phone startled her, causing her to jump and spill the hot coffee on her hand. Quickly she grabbed a towel and held it to her burning skin while the persistent ringing tested her patience. Jerking up the receiver, Leanne shouted, "Hello!"

"Leanne, where have you been? I . . ." She heard Bart's familiar voice come over the wire, bringing tears burning behind her eyes.

"I can't talk now, Bart," she managed to say before slamming the receiver, unable to confront him now, too humiliated even to let him know.

Again the phone rang, and she stared at it for some time before lifting the receiver and setting it down again.

Leanne slept fitfully, waking early, and hoping she only suffered from a nightmare. But the drawn features reflected in the bathroom mirror told her it had all been real. Bart had led her on and she had allowed him to. The shock was over; now what would she do? After a long, hot shower, Leanne emerged with a decision firmly planted in her mind; she would sell her home and move away. She didn't know where she would go, but she couldn't stay here knowing Bart would be living behind her.

Determined not to dwell on self-pity, Leanne forced herself to eat breakfast and dress. Rhonda would be coming in today, offering a pleasant distraction.

Leanne drove to the airport and tried to keep from thinking of Bart and the woman she had found in his apartment yesterday. She only hoped he wouldn't go to her parents with their problems. She maneuvered the car down the highway and off the ramp toward the airport parking lot. Already there were cars crowding the area, filling every available spot. She would be lucky if she could find a space, she thought, searching the parking lot. At last she parked the car and made her way to the lobby, where she checked the arriving flights.

Leanne was heading for the boarding gates when a familiar dark head caught her attention. The man was coming toward her, his head bent as he reached inside the pocket of his suit coat. Leanne stared, knowing it couldn't possibly be Bart. How would he have known she was here? No, it couldn't be him. But the man raised his head and hazel eyes burned into hers.

Bart picked up his pace, hurrying toward her as she swung around, frantically searching for a place to hide. She darted into a deserted hallway lined with pay phones, praying he wouldn't follow her. The hall was a dead end, and when she had gone as far as she could, she whirled around to face the large figure that stood between herself and freedom.

"What on earth is going on?" Bart asked, grabbing her arm when she tried to pass him. "Why wouldn't you talk to me last night?"

"I told you, I couldn't."

"And I want to know why. Is something wrong?"

"Bart, let me go," Leanne cried, his touch searing her flesh.

"I called to tell you that I wouldn't be able to get back until this morning," he said, ignoring her plea. "How did you know to meet me? I didn't get through to your parents, either." His eyes roamed her face. "You're shaking like a leaf. What's happened?" His voice was urgent, his grip on her tightening as a worried frown creased his brow. "The boys. Something's happened."

He didn't understand that she was not there to meet him. Leanne looked into his anxious face and shook her head. She had hoped not to see him again, at least not so soon. It was too much for her; she wanted to touch him, to hold him against her one more time. Reaching a trembling hand to the plane of his cheek, she held his gaze. "The boys are fine, Bart. I'm sure," she said, drinking in his good looks, making a mental picture of him so as to have it with her always. "They're probably at your apartment."

"Probably? Don't you know?" he asked, an angry glare replacing the concern.

Leanne withdrew her hand. How could she have been so stupid as to show him any affection? She struggled to free her arm of his grip, but it was useless.

"You're hurting me," she said through gritted teeth. Bart looked at the white knuckles of his hand on her arm and released her, watching as she rubbed her hand over the spot.

"What are you doing here, Leanne?" A clinking sound caused him to turn, and Leanne could see a man behind him placing coins into the pay phone near them. Bart turned his attention back to Leanne, his eyes narrow, his mouth a firm white line across his face as he waited for her answer. She couldn't believe it was less than a week ago that they had stood in this very hall. Bart had been so gentle, so loving.

Leanne shook herself mentally. He was not being gentle now and she wondered if loving was ever a term she could use in connection with him again.

"I'm waiting for an answer," Bart said impatiently.

"I'm here to pick up my cousin, remember?" Leanne tried to pass him again, but he stepped in front of her.

"What did you do, leave the boys to fend for themselves all night?" Bart growled.

"Of course not! I wouldn't do that," she said, hurt that he would think she would do such a thing.

"Flight two-ninety-eight from San Francisco now arriving at gate four," a voice sounded over the public-address system.

"I've got to go," she cried, pushing past Bart and running away from the hateful glare in his hazel eyes. The line of people moved fast, and soon she stepped through the metal detector and into the concourse, turning once to see Bart still watching her, his eyes still burning with anger. A knot formed in her throat, and she turned to keep him from seeing the tears that were beginning to fall. It was all backward. He was angry with her when she should still be angry with him, and she felt guilty when she was guiltless.

After finding gate four, Leanne stood near the windows. Staring at the broad wing of a jet, she remembered the anger in Bart's eyes. He would never forgive her for not keeping the children. If their relationship hadn't been over before, it certainly was over now. Well, Leanne thought, sniffing and wiping her eyes with a hanky, he could just have Blondie, and *she* could be the mother that Mathew and Charlie needed so badly.

A man's voice came over the intercom, reminding passengers of a departing flight. Closing her eyes, Leanne tried to get control of her emotions before she saw Rhonda, but the lump in her throat had grown larger and she sobbed quietly, knowing she would never be the mother or the wife she had dreamed of only twenty-four hours ago.

Leanne swallowed hard. It had been only five days since she had worried about Bart asking her to marry him, and now she ached with the knowledge that he never would. Leanne wanted to shake herself. Fool! she thought, hating herself for being so naive.

The smell of tobacco stirred her memories and her emotions. Turning, she found that the man next to her had lit a cigarette. Leanne walked away because the smoke reminded her of Bart.

Finally, a door opened admitting passengers from the San Francisco flight. Fighting off the tears, Leanne prepared herself to see Rhonda. She had decided not to tell her about Bart, but now she wasn't sure she could keep from it. She needed to confide in someone and Rhonda could be depended on to understand, unless she had changed.

Soon, Leanne saw the bouncy redheaded figure of her cousin, standing out in the crowd, a smile on her full, glossy lips. A feeling of relief filled Leanne as well-manicured hands reached for her and tanned arms hugged her close. Rhonda hadn't changed one bit. She was still the glamorous but sweet girl Leanne had grown up with, only now she wasn't a girl anymore, she was a beautiful woman.

"I can't believe I'm actually here," Rhonda said, linking her arm through Leanne's as they headed for the elevators. "It's been over two years," she added as they stepped into the privacy of an empty elevator.

Suddenly, Rhonda frowned and slanted her pretty head. "Something wrong?" she asked. The elevator opened to a crowd of people before Leanne could answer.

Grateful for the time it took to get the luggage, Leanne used the opportunity to pull herself together before Rhonda could get her alone again. However, when they had placed the suitcases in the car and were headed down the busy highway, the subject was not brought up. Instead, Rhonda asked about Leanne's mother and father.

"They're fine," Leanne answered, knowing Rhonda had missed her own parents. "Aunt Neecie and Uncle Ken are fine, too," Leanne added and glanced at her before returning her eyes to the road.

"You know they've never forgiven me for moving so far away."

"They just love you, Rhonda. You are their only child and . . ." Leanne paused. "Well," she said with a laugh, "I guess I know how that feels."

Rhonda joined her laughter. "I guess old K.H. will get over it when he discovers what a successful lawyer his little girl has turned out to be."

"Yeah, but did you have to move all the way out to California to prove you could do it?" Leanne asked, making a face.

"Well, not to prove that, but to prove something else . . . to myself."

Leanne maneuvered the car off one highway and onto another. "By the way, you didn't say how long you can stay. Two weeks, at least?" There was a hopeful lilt to her voice.

"Not exactly," Rhonda answered. "I'm actually here on business. In fact, we've got a party to go to this evening."

"You're kidding!" Leanne exclaimed before pulling into her aunt's driveway. "Where?"

"One of my newest affluent clients." Rhonda dramatized the words, making Leanne laugh.

Rhonda's mother and Sharon Masterson had made lunch for them all and as they talked, Leanne helped Rhonda unpack her clothes. The rest of the afternoon was spent getting ready for the party and reminiscing about good times. Rhonda had brought the latest fashions in shoes as well as clothes, and she gave Leanne free rein.

"This is like old times." Leanne giggled as Rhonda handed her a deep purple blouse with a plunging neckline. "Rhonda, you've always been a sharp dresser. How many times have I said you should be a model?"

"Plenty, but right now, I'm telling you to model. So hop to it and try that on." She pointed a slender finger in the direction of the blouse. "Wait," she said, turning back to the closet. "Here are the slacks." Leanne watched as Rhonda pulled a pair of shiny pants off a hanger and held them up. The legs tapered to the ankle, where they snapped.

"Oh, no, you don't, Rhonda." Leanne laughed, holding out one hand in mock defense. "You're not getting me into this outfit."

"Oh, yes, I am!" The dark eyes of her cousin danced with mischief. "What you need is a change in your life."

Leanne looked at her cousin's smiling face. What a

mind reader she was. "Maybe you should be a fortune-teller instead of a model," she said, snatching the pants from her cousin. "This will be a change, all right. From purchasing agent to clown! I hope no one I know will see me!"

Rhonda planted her hands on her shapely hips. "I'll have you know, young lady, that those are in style this season."

"Yeah. Well, so are swimming pools, but I don't see you wearing one!"

Rhonda grabbed a pillow off the bed and threw it at Leanne, who was already reaching for her own. The tension of the past few days was alleviated by the genuine fun Leanne enjoyed as she stepped back in time. She was a teenager again. Eric never existed, and Bart . . . Bart would always be there somewhere in the back of her mind, but for the moment his memory was only a dull aching in her heart.

The party, which turned out to be an elaborate barbecue, was given by a delightful couple who had a knack for creating a carefree atmosphere where everyone felt comfortable though there were several people who, like Leanne, didn't know many of the other guests.

Leanne lost her inhibitions about wearing the pants, but the soft skin exposed by the scooped neckline of the blouse made her self-conscious. She was used to the jeans and T-shirts she always wore at home. A smile curved her finely penciled lips. Bart had been surprised the first time he had taken her out. He was such a character, acting as though he were at the wrong address. Suddenly her smile began to quiver, and

Leanne reprimanded herself. She had to forget Bart. He belonged to Laura and probably always had.

A small group had gathered around the pool, listening to records, while others played charades. Rhonda was trying to act out the name of a movie. Feeling the desire for privacy, Leanne strolled outside, passing the pool, walking toward a gazebo where the lighting was soft and the music barely reached her.

Curling her hand around a tall white pole, Leanne swung around it. Leaning against the latticework of the half wall, she looked up at the stars, barely visible through the bright lights of the city. A siren could be heard in the distance, reminding Leanne of when she lived in Tulsa before moving to the country. Suddenly, she realized how much she loved her little home and the solitude that she knew there. She couldn't sell it and run away as Rhonda had. Bart would be her neighbor soon and she had to accept that. Even if it meant accepting Laura. "Oh God," she whispered. "Lord Jesus help me." Tears flowed freely down her cheeks as Leanne surrendered her pain and confusion, giving it to the Lord to handle, because she couldn't.

Now she understood what Rhonda had wanted to prove to herself. She had to prove she could make it on her own. Leanne hoped Rhonda would find what she was looking for and she would pray for her cousin, but she knew her own searching had led her to trust Christ and without Him she couldn't make it. Even now, though something inside her had died, she had to trust Him to replace it. With what, she didn't know, because there was nothing that could take Bart's place. But somehow Christ would pull her back together and she would go on with her life. She had to.

Chapter Nine

As Leanne dabbled her toes in the cool water of the creek, a good feeling inside of her made her wonder why she had ever felt the need to move. Everything she needed was here—quiet, peace and fresh air, unhampered by smog and traffic sounds. It was the last day of her vacation, and she was looking forward to going back to work tomorrow.

Hugging her knees, Leanne allowed her gaze to travel across the creek to the unfinished cabin. Bart must have decided he didn't want to be around her this summer and thus called off construction for the time being. A coldness had settled inside her. She had cried all the tears that there were to be cried, and now all she could do was to accept what life had dealt her, knowing God would work it out for her good.

Standing, Leanne ran her fingers through the short

crop of curls that barely touched her shoulders. How Rhonda had talked her into cutting her hair she had no idea. She had wanted a change, and Rhonda had made sure she got it. Her father had been so mad that he had refused to talk to her at first; then all he could do was complain about Rhonda and her crazy, wild schemes. Her mother had liked it but didn't say so in front of her husband. Stephen was the only one so far who had genuinely complimented her on it. Who cares, she thought, walking back to the house. Rhonda had been right. It did give her a new outlook. She felt sophisticated and sure of herself. She didn't know if it was the hairdo or the devil-may-care attitude she had adopted.

The telephone was ringing when she entered the house and, expecting it to be Stephen, she grabbed the receiver. "Hello," she said cheerfully.

"Leanne, you're home." Leanne froze. She couldn't mistake the voice. It was Bart. "I've been trying to reach you all day." Leanne heard him speaking, but she was too stunned to reply or even hang up. How could she have thought she was over him? Just the sound of his voice flooded her with memories she had so carefully tucked away. "I'm in Texas now, but I'll be back in the morning. Have lunch with me tomorrow."

"No!" Leanne said. Her instincts told her to hang up, but she couldn't.

"I need to talk to you, Leanne."

"Well, I don't want to talk to you." She breathed deeply as her voice began to shake. "Bart, I don't have anything to say to you and I think you've said enough."

"I'll pick you up at twelve-thirty, Leanne. I said I have to talk to you, and I intend to do just that." The dial tone followed a quick click of the receiver, and

Leanne sat down, holding the phone in her lap. What was she going to do? Seeing him again would be worse than merely hearing his voice, and that had been hard enough.

Leanne played with the buttons of her jacket while she waited impatiently for Stephen to return to his office. It was twelve, but she felt sure that Bart would show up early. Stephen had agreed to take her out to lunch so that she wouldn't be there when Bart came, but if he didn't hurry, she was going to leave without him. Pacing the floor, she stared at the navy straps of her sandals, the crisscross pattern hypnotizing her. Then, leaning against the arm of a massive leather chair, she traced the navy pinstripes of her skirt and sighed. The door opened and Stephen rushed into the room.

"Sorry that took so long. Are you ready?" he asked, shuffling papers on his desk.

"Yes," Leanne said as she picked up her handbag and started for the door, turning to be sure Stephen was following her. Instead, he was filing papers.

"I'll be just a minute more," he said, apology in his voice.

"Please, Stephen," Leanne pleaded with him as she moved to the desk, taking his arm, physically urging him to hurry.

"All right, all right." He laughed and allowed her to maneuver him toward the door.

However, before they reached the door, a commotion could be heard on the other side, and soon Bart burst into the room with Stephen's secretary furiously following him. "I'm sorry, Mr. Carlile. He just . . ."

"Thank you, Vicky." Stephen excused her and the secretary left the room, closing the door behind her. "What are you doing here?" he asked Bart. Hazel eyes bore into Leanne's green ones, causing her to pull away from Stephen and move across the room.

Bart ignored Stephen's question and followed Leanne. "What did you do to your hair?" he asked, his gaze taking in the soft curls around her face. Leanne glared at him. How dare he question her actions! He had his nerve!

"Never mind that," Bart continued. "Why didn't you at least let me know that Laura had Mathew and Charlie? Why did you let me accuse you of deserting them?" he demanded.

Stephen moved next to Leanne. "I think you have some explaining of your own to do, Bart. Leanne—"

"This is none of your business, Carlile! Leanne, can't we talk privately?" Bart asked, impatience in his voice.

"I don't think that's a good idea," Stephen said, resting against the desk as if to say he wasn't leaving.

Leanne watched Bart clench and unclench his fists. "Please, Stephen," she said, stepping between the two men.

"Sure you'll be all right?" he asked, rising to his feet.

"Yes, Stephen, I'm sure."

"All right? Of course you'll be all right! What does he think I'm going to do to you?" Bart asked, his jaw tightening as he watched Stephen leave the room. When they were alone, he searched Leanne's face, his anger melting, replaced by the unnerving smile that belonged to him alone. "What's going on, angel?" he asked softly, stepping closer to her. "Laura said you just stormed out, leaving her to keep Mathew and

Charlie. I don't understand. It isn't like you to get so upset over some petty jealousy."

Leanne choked back tears that threatened to fall. *Petty jealousy!* How dare he think that of her! Turning away from Bart, she faced the window behind her. Pigeons cooed on the ledges of the old buildings. The street was packed with cars. On the sidewalks, people were laughing as they hurriedly stopped at first one window, then the next. Their lives were going on naturally while hers was falling apart. Closing her eyes to the world around her, Leanne prayed silently for the strength she so desperately needed. Her eyes fluttered open as she felt Bart behind her, his touch searing through the material of her jacket into the flesh of her arms. His voice was low, whispering into the feathery softness of her hair. "Don't worry, angel. We'll work it out."

Leanne's green eyes darted furiously, her arms folded across her chest, nails digging into her skin as she turned around to face him. "What do you think I am?" she demanded, her voice calmer than she imagined it could be. "I'm not a fool, Bart."

"I don't know what you're talking about, but the boys are crazy about you, and you can't just walk out of their lives like this!"

Leanne knew that he was right, but she couldn't think with him so close, his breath mingling with hers. Somehow she would have to make it up to Mathew and Charlie, but right now she had to get away from Bart. "I don't want to see you again, Bart," she said in controlled tones, staring defiantly into his eyes before walking out of the room while he swore he would never understand women.

Leanne no longer felt pain, only fury. The crying was over, but a raging anger had taken its place. She found Stephen waiting for her in the lobby and determinedly walked up to him. "If we had left when I said we should, none of this would have happened. We would have been gone before he got here!"

"Calm down, Leanne," Stephen said, glancing around at the curious customers who were listening to her rave. Taking her arm, he said, "Let's go now."

"Now is too late," she said, pulling away from him. "I will take myself to lunch, thank you." She stormed out of the store and down the sidewalk, not caring which direction she took. She shouldn't have taken her anger out on Stephen that way, but it was true. He had delayed her escape.

Deciding that she didn't really want lunch, Leanne headed instead toward a local park. There, she watched children playing on swings and squealing as they sailed down the slippery slides. She strolled along the edge of a flower garden and across a wooden bridge, where she stopped to watch ducks splashing in the water, sticking their tails in the air while their long necks stretched below the surface to catch minnows. She had calmed down considerably by the time she returned to work, and, finding Stephen sulking in his office, she apologized.

"I understand," Stephen said. "Now let me make my blundering up to you by taking you to dinner and a movie."

"I've told you, it wasn't your fault, Stephen. You don't have to make anything up to me." Seeing his face drop Leanne added, "But . . . you can take me to dinner simply because I'm such good company, can't you?" She smiled a pretty smile, flashing her dark lashes at him.

Stephen laughed, leaning back in his chair. "You are something else, Miss Masterson. Where would you like to eat?" he asked as he leaned forward against the desk. "Chinese food okay?"

"That sounds good. What's playing at the cinema?"

"I have a brilliant idea. Instead of a movie, we could go to the Little Theater. There's a new company in town, and they're doing *Annie Get Your Gun*. With the mood you were in earlier, I thought you had gone to get yours!"

Leanne laughed. "Was I that bad?" she asked, making a face.

"Don't I look like a man who thought he had lost his best friend?"

"Oh, Stephen. You didn't!"

"Yes, I did. The way you stormed out of here, I thought I'd not only lost my best friend, but a valued employee as well."

"Does this mean I get a raise?" she teased.

"Ha-ha!" Stephen laughed. "You just got a raise."

Smiling, Leanne said slyly, "I did, didn't I? In that case, I'd better get back to work." Leaning across the desk, Leanne tapped his hand. "Seriously, Stephen. Thank you for always being here for me."

"Just don't forget it next time," he said, winking a brown eye.

"I won't, I promise," she said, crossing her heart dramatically.

"I'll pick you up at six," he called to her as she opened the door.

Leanne went back to her office, feeling content with

her life. She was not by any means happy, thanks to Bart, but she was able to laugh, if not in private, at least with others. Stephen was a true friend. With him, she could laugh as well as cry. She could yell at him and still he loved her. Sitting at her desk, she stared blankly at the paperweight in front of her. It was a shame that she and Stephen didn't get together. They got along so well, and he was a wonderful guy. He would make a good husband, she thought, clicking the tip of her ball-point up and down. But their relationship wasn't like that and never would be.

Leanne busied herself with checking the list of new merchandise she had to order and making calls to the suppliers. The afternoon wore on slowly, and it was all she could do to concentrate on her work. Bart's smiling face kept materializing in front of her and his words rang in her ears. "We'll work it out," she said aloud, imitating Bart. "I wonder what day of the week he would have been mine!" Moving to the window, she chewed the end of her pen as she watched the activity in the street below her. "He would have never been mine! He would have been Laura's, as he is now!" Leanne cried as she whirled around, slinging the pen across the room.

Leanne was looking forward to seeing Chan, the owner of the small Chinese restaurant where she and Stephen always went when they wanted won ton and steak kew. Her stomach growled at the thought as she ran a brush through her silky hair.

But on the way to the restaurant, she noticed that Stephen was heading in the wrong direction. "Where are you going, Stephen? Chan's place is in the other direction, or did you forget?"

"I didn't forget. I'm not taking you to Chan's. You've never been to the Paper Dragon, and I think it's about time I took you somewhere really nice. You deserve a better atmosphere than Chan's after what you've been through lately."

Leanne's breath caught in her throat. She *had* been to the Paper Dragon, and she didn't want to go back, not yet. But she would have to brave the memory of that first real date with Bart or chance making Stephen feel bad, and she had done enough of that this morning. Stephen rambled on about how much she would like the restaurant as well as the food.

"The preparation of the food is done right in front of you at your table," he was saying while she listened with false eagerness. "Actually, it's very entertaining. You've never seen anything like it," he went on. The neon sign advertising the restaurant came into view and Leanne steeled herself against any tears that might be waiting to fall.

They passed through the private tables as she and Bart had done, and entered the wide area where they were seated at one of the horseshoe-shaped tables in the back of the room. When the maître d' left them, Stephen turned to Leanne, who was staring at another table where a chef had already started his show.

"Like it?" he asked hopefully.

Leanne didn't answer him but continued to stare at the table across the room. A couple with two children sat alone, and though the room was dimly lit, she was sure it was Bart with Mathew and Charlie, and of course the woman would be Laura. Stephen followed her gaze and sighed heavily. "I'm really sorry, Leanne. I had no idea. This was supposed to get your mind off the creep."

Leanne looked at Stephen and smiled. "I'm all right, really. Don't worry. It will be fun, I'm sure. You were right," she said, looking around the room at the various Oriental objects that decorated the large area. "This place has a lot more atmosphere than Chan's." It was true, but she longed to be in the old familiar restaurant with its butcher-block tables and Chan's smiling face, making them feel like the only patrons in the place.

A bright light shone at Bart's table, attracting her attention, and she was able to see his face more clearly. His eyes were on the grill in front of him, but he seemed preoccupied until Mathew grabbed his arm, squealing with delight. Bart turned to his son and the blond beauty next to him, flashing her a broad smile. The bright light faded, and along with it went Leanne's vow to be strong. That special smile—it was for her at one time, now it would be Laura's. Even Mathew and Charlie seemed to be enjoying themselves, giggling at everything the woman said. They looked like a family out for the evening. Someday they would be, Leanne thought regretfully, turning as another couple joined her and Stephen. A chef brought his cart to their table, and for Stephen's sake as well as her own she avoided looking in Bart's direction, pretending to be genuinely interested and surprised by the chef's display.

The show was over and they were eating when Leanne heard Mathew calling her name. "Miss Leanne. There's Miss Leanne, Dad."

Looking up, Leanne saw Mathew and Charlie skip

over to the table, Laura and Bart following them a little reluctantly.

"Hi, Miss Leanne! Where've you been?" Mathew asked, coming to her side, extending a small arm to hug her.

Leanne put her arm around the boy and smiled at Charlie. "Hello, Mathew. Charlie. How have you been?" she asked, trying to sound happy to see them.

"We haven't seen you in a long time, Miss Leanne," Charlie stated. Being older, he probably sensed the trouble between herself and his father, and was using more tact than Mathew in asking where she had been.

"I've been kinda busy, boys, but I've missed you both very much."

"Leanne has had company from California," Bart said as he joined them. "But maybe now she will have time to help decorate our new cabin," he added, coaxing the boys to invite her, his eyes holding hers as he spoke.

"I don't think I will have ti—"

"Oh, please, Miss Leanne," Mathew begged.

Leanne shot Bart an angry glare but found it didn't faze him at all. "We really do need your help. I'm color-blind, and somebody has to help us pick curtains." His hazel eyes sparkled in the light of the candle on the table and Leanne felt herself being drawn back into the world she had loved. Only the blond woman standing quietly in the background kept her from giving in to the tempting invitation.

"Laura could help you," she said. "And I'm sure she would do a better job than I would."

"Laura has a whole house to decorate and I doubt she would have the time," Bart said, turning to smile at

Laura, who stood holding her clutch bag under her arm, a smug smile across her pink lips.

Of course, Leanne thought. She gets the house, I get a weekend cabin. Only typical of the sort of life that she would be letting herself in for if she were to marry Bart, which she wasn't about to do. "I don't know," she finally said to the waiting faces before her. Desperately, she looked at Stephen.

"Leanne will be pretty busy herself at the store. We've got a lot of work coming up."

Bart watched Leanne's face lighten with relief. "If that's how you feel, Leanne," he said, his eyes boring into hers. "We'll manage, I'm sure." Bart turned to walk away, but Mathew's words stopped him.

"Come on, Miss Leanne. Please? It will be funner if you would help."

Leanne looked into the pitiful eyes of the freckle-faced boy and was about to give in when his father called him. "Don't bother Leanne anymore, Matt," he said, glancing in her direction. "She's busy." With those words, he stalked out of the restaurant, with Laura and the children following him.

"I tell you what gets to me," Stephen began when they were alone. "And that's how that Laura can put up with his open pursuit of you."

"I don't know," Leanne said, shaking her head in utter frustration. "I don't know and I don't care." Scooting her chair back, she added, "If you're finished, I'm ready for the theater. I could use a good laugh right now." Leanne left the table, not caring if the other couple had heard the entire conversation, not caring if Stephen followed her or not. She only wanted to free herself of the pain that had crept into her heart against her will.

The actors at that evening's performance played their parts well and the script overflowed with comedy. However, the laughter Leanne wanted never came; there was only a growing bitterness that she couldn't get rid of. As Stephen drove her home she wondered how she could have even considered helping with the cabin. It was Mathew's pleading that had softened her resolve. He didn't understand what was going on, and Bart's abrupt departure hadn't helped matters. Leanne toyed absently with the long bow on the front of her white blouse. Now Mathew and Charlie would think she was too busy for them. Wasn't that what she had been trying to say? Leanne asked herself. Sighing heavily, she turned to look out the window next to her. The darkness was all she could see until Stephen pulled onto her road and scattered streetlights revealed the edge of the wide fields that surrounded them.

"It was really fun, Stephen," Leanne said when he pulled into her drive. "Thanks for taking me."

"It's okay, Leanne," Stephen said, shutting off the engine. "You don't have to pretend with me. It was horrible for you, and I know it." Stephen reached across her to open her door before opening his own. "Make me a cup of coffee and I'll keep you company for a while," he said, getting out of the car.

"That isn't necessary, Stephen," she said over the top of the car when she had gotten out, slamming the door closed.

Stephen leaned his arms against the hood of the car

and played with his keys. "I guess you'd rather be alone."

"Actually," Leanne admitted, shrugging her shoulders, "I really would. I appreciate your offer, though. Maybe next time, okay?"

"Sure," Stephen said, climbing into his seat. "I'll see you tomorrow. Unless you think you need the day off?"

Leanne had walked over to his side of the car and now lowered her head to see in his window. "You're a terrific friend, Stephen, but a terrible businessman. I'll be there tomorrow; thanks, anyway." Stephen started the engine and Leanne watched as he backed out of the driveway and onto the road.

The night was warm and, walking toward the red-wood deck, she slipped out of the jacket, untying the bow of her blouse and loosening the first few buttons before relaxing on a lounge chair. Letting her head drop against the back of the chair, she stared up into the sky. The stars were bright and the moon hung among them majestically. Crickets sang in the distance, and occasionally a frog would plop into the creek.

Poor Stephen, she thought, laughing halfheartedly. He had tried so hard to cheer her up. If the evening hadn't been so painful, it would have been funny. She thought she had known Bart. She'd thought he was gentle. He had promised never to hurt her, and she had believed him. That was a joke!

"I knew better!" she said through gritted teeth, slamming her hand against the arm of the chair, the action stinging her palm. The clear night air carried the sound of a familiar deep chuckle from the creek, and suddenly she stood, staring across the yard toward the water. The porch light was blinding her, so she stepped off the deck. There was the silhouette of a man standing with his feet apart and his arms folded across his chest, facing her from the other side of the creek.

This was the second time Bart had waited for her to come home, and she was furious. Determinedly she made her way across the soft grass to the old bridge. The figure moved and a light flashed in front of his face. He was lighting a cigarette, nonchalantly waiting for her. He won't feel so carefree when I'm finished with him, she thought, crossing the bridge with no consideration for the consequences if her heels slipped on the log. Once she'd reached the other side, she faced Bart bravely.

"What do you think you are doing, spying on me?" she blurted out, her hands on her hips and her chin thrust forward. "I don't intend to put up with this. You are harassing me, and I won't stand for it!" she finished, folding her arms defiantly.

"Harassing you?" Bart said, laughter in his voice. "I was minding my own business, enjoying the quiet evening, when you come stomping over here to attack me."

"I didn't *attack*—" Leanne started.

"But you'd like to, wouldn't you?" Bart interrupted her, drawing on his cigarette as he watched her face turn violet. Even in the dark, the color could be seen as it rushed to her face.

"You're despicable, Bart Hall!" she screamed at him, her anger getting out of control. "I want to know what you are doing here!"

"On my own property?" he asked, tossing his cigarette into the creek. "I'm not the one trespassing, you are!" Mischief danced in his eyes as a smile curved his lips. His magnetism was drawing her forward, but, determined to fight, Leanne lashed out at him, her arm caught in midair by his powerful hand. Before she had time to object, he had drawn her into his arms, his embrace draining her of her anger as he always could do.

Afraid of her own weakness, Leanne pushed his hands aside. "Please, Bart," she whispered, willing him to stop but wanting him to continue. His hands moved to her arms, lifting her into the kiss that awaited her as she stood on her tiptoes, leaning against his hard frame. Her arms found their way around his waist, where they clung, pulling her still closer to him.

He released her lips and laid his head against her small shoulder. "Don't ever leave me, Leanne," he whispered, his breath tickling her neck. "I need you here in my arms, where you belong."

Something in his words made Leanne grow cold. What about Laura? Pulling away from him, she looked into his puzzled eyes. "It will never work, Bart," she whispered breathlessly before she fled for the solitude of her house.

Chapter Ten

Weeks passed, and Leanne hadn't heard from Bart or seen him, though construction on the cabin across the creek had begun again. She was walking up the slope to her parents' home when she heard the sound of children's laughter. Reaching the top of the hill, she could see Mathew and Charlie under a tree at the side of the house wrestling with Pepper, the black-and-white rat terrier that had been hers before she left home. The old dog loved to wrestle despite her age, and Leanne lingered to watch her wriggle in and out of a tangle of arms and legs as the boys rolled about on the ground. "Charlie . . ." she heard her mother's voice call. "Mathew . . ."

Leanne started back down the hill, hoping to escape unseen, but Mathew caught sight of her. "Miss Leanne!" he called, scrambling to his feet and running in her direction.

Reluctantly, she stopped and turned around. "Hello, Mathew," she said, kneeling to accept his hug. Suddenly Charlie and Pepper ran into them, sending them all to the ground in a heap of thrashing limbs. "No, Pepper, no!" Leanne laughed as the dog ran in circles about their heads. Freeing her arms from under Mathew and Charlie, she grabbed at the speckled pest as she whizzed by. "You silly old dog. Don't you know you're too old to be acting like that?" Sitting up and crossing her jeans-clad legs in front of her, Leanne hugged Pepper to her chest, the dog's lolling tongue continually licking Leanne's neck and chin. Mathew and Charlie giggled and pushed her to the ground on her back, tickling her, while Pepper ran from one boy to another, barking hysterically.

"Lea! I might have known." The stern voice caused the laughing group to freeze, and Leanne looked up to see her mother wiping her hands on an apron, a cheerful smile on her soft face.

"Hi, Mom," she managed to say between gasps for air. She sat up, running her fingers through her short curls, pulling out twigs and blades of grass. "These stinkers are murder," she said, reaching over to tweak Charlie's nose.

"Tell me about it. I've been trying to get them in to dinner for the past fifteen minutes. Now get washed up, you two," she said to the boys, slapping her hands together. "Pronto!" she added teasingly as they raced toward the house.

Leanne stood, brushing her pants off as she walked with her mother. She had been so caught up in the roughhousing that she hadn't even thought of Bart being there until his tall figure appeared at the screen door. "I really can't stay, Mom. I've—"

"I know," Mrs. Masterson interrupted her. "But you at least have time for dinner. You have to eat, and besides, that's why you came up, isn't it?" she added, taking her daughter's arm and propelling her toward the screen door, where Bart still stood.

"What do you mean, you know?" Leanne asked as they neared the house.

"Well, Bart told us how busy you've been. Of course, we figured that, since you hadn't been up to the house in a while. But anyway," she went on as they approached the steps, "he said there was no need to bother you for dinner tonight, because he didn't think you would be able to come."

Bart opened the screen for them, and Leanne took the opportunity to glare at him as she passed by. "I'm glad to see I was wrong," he said, ignoring the face she made.

"I am, too," her mother said before leaving them alone in the foyer. "Dinner is ready, so don't dillydally out here too long," she called over her shoulder.

Leanne was furious. She had no intentions of dillydallying or anything else with Bart Hall. "I didn't know you were here, or I wouldn't have come," she said bitterly.

"Then I'm glad you didn't know," he replied, his hazel eyes beaming at her frustration. Unable to think of anything to say, Leanne whirled around to follow her mother.

"Hadn't we better go in together?" Bart asked.

"Why should we?" she snapped, turning to face him.

"I was under the impression that you didn't want your parents to know about our little tiff, or should I say *your* little tiff?"

Leanne was saved from answering him by her father's booming voice. "Hi, princess," he said, hugging her tight. "Your visits have been kinda scarce these days. I know you're a hard worker, but Carlile ought not to pressure you so much. Doesn't he know that all work and no play is no fun? Right, Bart?" He laughed, slapping Bart on the back and placing an arm across Leanne's shoulders, directing them to the dining room, where her mother had laid a scrumptious table. "Sunday dinner on Saturday," Rob Masterson said, taking his seat at the table and motioning for Leanne and Bart to do the same. "Bet you could smell your mother's homemade bread all the way to the creek, couldn't you, Leanne?" He watched the way she looked at Bart and took her flushed face for blushing. "Or was it knowing Bart was so close that brought you running up here?" he teased, a devilish smile curving his lips.

Leanne glanced across the table at Bart's smug smile. He was obviously enjoying the predicament she was in. If she had told her parents what had happened, she wouldn't have to play this ridiculous game.

"Where are Mathew and Charlie?" Sharon Masterson asked when she came into the dining room with a platter of fried chicken.

"They're just being boys, honey. Let them alone," her husband said.

"I'll check on them," Leanne said, grateful for an excuse to leave the room.

During dinner, Leanne's father talked about the local Indian tribes while Mathew and Charlie hung on his every word. Sharon Masterson shook her head, silently complaining of her husband's exaggerations. Leanne picked at the chicken on her plate, fighting to keep her mind off the man sitting opposite her, his presence driving her emotions to the brink of chaos. Through dark lashes she followed the print of the tablecloth to Bart's place setting and watched the powerful hands that rested on each side of his plate. The lean fingers of one curled around a tea glass, and as he lifted it to his lips Leanne allowed her gaze to follow it, noting the strong angle of his chin and his thick tanned neck. He lowered the glass, and she watched his firm lips press together before forming a smile, the deep line of his dimple creasing his rough cheek. How she loved him. Everything about him. She closed her eyes momentarily, then opened them to brave a glance into his hazel eyes but found he was watching her. Quickly she lowered her gaze to his chest for fear he would be able to read her thoughts.

The dark blue plaid shirt he wore open at the neck revealed a gold chain that glimmered in the light, a contrast to the dark hairs of his chest. Blinking, as if the action could erase her thoughts, Leanne turned to look at her father. Absently she played with the chain around her own neck while she half listened to him teasing Mathew and Charlie.

"Hey, princess," he said, directing his attention to her. "Where did you get that necklace?" Leanne glanced from her father down to the glass angel lying against her melon-colored shirt and covered it with her hand.

"I—" she started.

"That's the one that Bart gave her," Sharon

Masterson explained. "Don't you remember, Rob? She showed it to us that day she brought over our shell pictures from their trip to Galveston. The way those tiny shells are arranged into a picture . . ."

Leanne heard her mother's voice, but she wasn't listening to her words. She wished she had left the pendant tucked away in her jewelry box. She had put it on that morning while reminiscing about a time when she was happy. It had been a stupid thing to do, she thought, closing her hand around the cool glass and stealing a look at Bart from under her thick lashes. He wasn't listening to her mother, either. He was watching her, and with evident pleasure at knowing she still treasured his gift. She had worn it hidden under her shirt, but it must have come out when she was playing with Mathew and Charlie. She had forgotten that she even had it on. It was a wonder it hadn't broken.

Sharon Masterson turned to Bart, who was sitting next to her. "That really is a beautiful pendant, Bart, and you can't imagine how much it means to her."

Leanne's hand tightened around the angel, and as she applied the unintended pressure she felt the glass snap. Lowering her hand, she opened it to find the angel in her palm, the halo missing.

"Oh, no," her mother gasped.

Leanne looked up at the faces waiting for their reaction. There was pity in all their eyes, all except Bart's. He was looking away, hiding his expression from her. He thinks that I've broken it on purpose, she thought. Tears stung her eyes and, no matter how hard she tried, she was unable to keep her feelings in check. "Excuse me," she mumbled under her breath as she left the table, making her way through the open patio door.

Outside, the tears fell unashamedly down her flushed cheeks. Leaning against a tree, Leanne looked at the tiny object in her hand. Her heart ached as much for the loss of the gift as for what Bart must be thinking of her. She would have a lot of explaining to do tomorrow, but tonight she had to get away. Rounding the corner of the house, she ran into a hard object that knocked the breath out of her.

"I thought I'd find you on your way home," a familiar voice said as strong arms closed around her, giving support to her shaky legs. When she had regained her breath, Leanne pulled free of Bart's hold and headed across the front yard toward the shell road that would take her home. She could hear his heavy steps behind her and turned around to face him.

"I thought I told you to leave me alone!" she cried.

"You're a real puzzle, angel," he said softly, running the back of his hand over her smooth cheek.

"Don't call me that!" she cried, pushing his hand away.

His hand returned to brush her jawline as his eyes held hers, daring her to defy him again. He lifted the fine chain around her neck, the golden halo dangling between his fingers. "You still have your halo," he teased; the anger in his eyes had been replaced by his irresistible smile. Leanne stared up at him, her own anger dispersing as she anticipated his kiss. He lowered the chain easily, his fingers brushing the hollow of her neck as he did so. Leanne shivered and her heart beat wildly as his hazel eyes searched her green ones. Maybe she had lost her halo, because right now she only wanted Bart to take her in his arms, to make her forget everything but his touch.

But his kiss never came and he didn't take her in his arms. Instead, he shoved his hands into his pockets and walked past her.

Beside herself with embarrassment, Leanne felt her anger returning. *I don't believe this,* she thought. "Where do you think you're going?" she asked, running to catch up with him.

"Your parents are pretty worried. I told them I'd see that you were all right," he said as he continued to walk, his pace too fast for her. "So," he continued, "if you're going home, I'm walking you there."

Walking me or running me, she thought as she took two steps to his one. "If you'd just stay out of my life, I'd be fine!"

Bart looked down at her and slowed his pace, allowing her to walk more comfortably by his side. "If you want me out of your life so badly, then why did you tell your father he could play grandpa to Matt and Charlie?"

"I . . . that . . ." Leanne stammered, standing in front of Bart when he stopped to light a cigarette.

He watched her face through the flame of the lighter before lighting the end of the cigarette to an orange glow. "I don't think you really want me out of your life," he said as the smoke drifted into the night air.

"That's ridiculous."

"Then explain what your father told me."

Leanne could imagine just what her father had said and knew there was no explaining she could do that would convince Bart her father had exaggerated. "That was before I met Laura," she finally said.

"What has Laura got to do with us? I can't tell her just to forget—"

"And why not?" Leanne blurted, glad it was all out in the open.

Bart dropped his cigarette at his feet, crushing the fire out with his boot, intentionally taking his time to answer her. Leanne twisted her ring around her finger nervously. Over and over she turned it, anxious for the answer he would give. Finally his eyes met hers, and even in the dark she could see a change in his expression. It was a serious look that caused a knot to form in her throat. "If you love me, Leanne," he began, his eyes searching her face, "you'll leave Laura out of this."

Leanne's heart sank. Anger was her only defense against the tears that she fought to control. "And what makes you think I love you?" she asked, laughing a little shakily. Before her words could register, she turned away, walking carelessly into the driveway that led to her house. When she reached the redwood deck, she pulled out her keys, thankful for the absence of Bart's footsteps behind her.

Somehow Leanne made it through the next few weeks without falling completely apart. She hadn't seen Bart or the boys since that night she had broken her necklace. Her parents must have sensed trouble between them and hadn't asked about Bart again. Bart could have told them for her, chivalrous as he was, she thought as she filed away a stack of purchase orders. It was early afternoon and she already wanted to go home. There wouldn't be many days of warm weather left, and she would rather spend them on the creek bank than in a concrete office.

Shoving the file drawer into place, she strolled over to the window. Fall colors were already claiming their place on the trees in the park. School had started and the swings and slides sat vacant all day, waiting for three o'clock when the park again would come alive with children's laughter. Bart must have decided she meant what she said, because he hadn't even been out to the new cabin.

The telephone rang, and Leanne went back to her desk to answer it. "Hello," she said when she lifted the receiver.

"Miss Masterson?" a strange woman's voice said from the other end. "Miss Leanne Masterson?"

"Yes?" Leanne replied, wondering who would be calling her directly.

"This is Patricia Peckat, the school nurse over at Taylor Elementary."

"Yes," Leanne said again, anxious for the woman to get to the point of her call.

"I have Mathew Hall in my office and he insisted that we call you. We haven't been able to reach his father and the emergency number we have is out of order."

"What's wrong with Mathew, Ms. Peckat?"

"Nothing really serious; he has an upset stomach and a rash has broken out on his chest. Probably measles. His fever is slight, so I don't think there's anything to worry about."

"Doesn't Mr. Hall have a housekeeper or someone else you could call? I'm not sure I can get away."

Leanne was desperate for an excuse not to get involved with Bart again. She had finally been able to stop crying herself to sleep, and she knew that another confrontation would just open the floodgates again.

"Well, Miss Masterson, Mr. Olsen, our school principal, didn't want to call you to begin with. He tried to explain to Mathew that since your name wasn't one of those listed as an emergency number, we couldn't call you. But Mathew insisted that if his father or grandmother couldn't be reached he wanted you and wouldn't go with anyone else." There was a pause, and then the woman said, "I'm sorry to bother you, Miss Masterson. Mathew will just have to accept the help of his housekeeper. Thank you—"

"Wait," Leanne interrupted her before she could hang up. "How did you get my number if it wasn't on your list?"

"Mathew gave it to us. He has it written on the inside covers of all his notebooks."

"My work number?" Leanne asked, finding it hard to believe.

"That and your home number."

Leanne was touched. She didn't know if Bart or Charlie was responsible for helping him find her number, but she felt compelled to go to Mathew. "Tell Matt that I'm on my way." Hanging up the receiver, Leanne grabbed the forest green jacket off her chair and headed for the door, digging into her purse for her keys as she went. What could possibly happen? she told herself as she started the car. I'll just drop him off with the housekeeper and make sure he gets settled, then I'll leave. Driving to the school, she assured herself that there was no way she could run into Bart.

She was still trying to convince herself that she was doing the right thing when she pulled into the parking lot of Bart's apartment house. As she and Mathew waited for the elevator a horrible thought crossed her mind. What about Laura? What if Laura were to show up? Her stomach was in knots when they stood in front of the apartment door waiting for the housekeeper to let them in.

When the door opened, Leanne was faced with the kindly blue eyes of the housekeeper and knew that she would at least have an ally if trouble came. The woman thought the world of Mathew and was terribly upset that the school hadn't called her. She insisted that Leanne let her repay her for bringing him home. A slice of blueberry pie and fresh coffee was hard to resist, so Leanne allowed herself the luxury of being in Bart's home a little longer.

It wasn't long before Charlie came in from school wanting to know what happened to Mathew, full of excited expectations concerning Leanne's presence. "You are going to stay and eat supper with us, aren't you, Miss Leanne?" he asked, dropping his books onto the kitchen table while he dug into the cookie jar.

"I don't think so, Charlie. Matter of fact, I need to be going right now." Leanne looked at her watch and wondered when Bart would come in.

"But you've got to, Miss Leanne. Mathew's real sick, and I know he wants you to stay with him. Besides, Mrs. Winters needs to go home early today, don't you, Mrs. Winters?"

Leanne glanced at the housekeeper, who looked eager to have the evening off. "I wish I could," Leanne said, taking Charlie's chin in her palm, looking into his pleading eyes. He reminded her so much of his father.

"You can!" Mathew said.

Leanne turned around to see Mathew leaning against the doorframe. "What are you doing out of bed, Mathew?"

"You have to stay. Charlie said you were still my friend, and if I needed you, to call, and you would come."

"Of course I'm still your friend, and I did come, Mathew," Leanne said, going to his side, placing her hand to his warm face. "But I really shouldn't stay."

"You see," Charlie said. "She said *shouldn't*. That means she can."

"You boys don't give Miss Masterson any more trouble, now. She says she can't stay, and so she can't," Mrs. Winters said as she opened the oven door to check on a roast.

"Thank you, Mrs. Winters," Leanne said. Mathew began to cry softly. "Don't cry, Mathew, please? You'll be fine with Mrs. Winters and Charlie." Leanne looked to the housekeeper for support, but the woman ignored the situation and kept peeling the potatoes into the sink in front of her. Turning back to Mathew, she said, "Your dad will be home soon."

"You don't really have to leave, do you, Miss Leanne?" Charlie asked, his grown-up voice putting her on the spot.

"I . . ." Leanne looked from Charlie's accusing face to Mathew's tearstained one. Sighing, she turned again to the housekeeper, who never looked up from her work. "Really, boys," she finally said, pleading with them to understand. Neither of them changed expression. Leanne was torn between staying and facing Bart when he came home, and leaving Charlie angry and Mathew in tears. "Oh all right, I'll stay."

"All right!" Charlie grinned, lifting his fist into the air as a sign of victory. Mathew simply smiled weakly and clung to her.

"That will be really nice," Mrs. Winters said, looking up from the sink, a smile on her face. "I'll just finish dinner and leave you guys alone. Mr. Hall will be in soon, and won't he be glad to see you here." It was a statement, not a question, and Leanne wondered just how much Mrs. Winters knew about her relationship with Bart. If it hadn't been for Mathew's rash and fever, she would have sworn it was all a conspiracy.

Mrs. Winters kept her word, and after finishing the vegetables, she left, saying the roast would be finished in another hour. Leanne played a game with Charlie while Mathew rested on the couch. Only half of her attention was on the game, as she constantly expected Bart to come home. She knew his job required extended hours, but Mrs. Winters had said he would be in soon. "But how soon?"

"What'd you say?" Charlie asked, gaining her full attention.

"I'm sorry, Charlie. Were you talking to me?"

Charlie laughed. "You said something first."

"Oh. Well, I was just talking to myself. Is it my turn?" she asked, trying to change the subject.

The telephone rang and Charlie picked up the receiver. "Hello," he said. "Oh, hi, Dad." Charlie winked at Leanne and pointed to the receiver. Leanne shook her head, frowning. She certainly didn't want to talk to

Bart. Absently she doodled on the score pad while she listened to Charlie's end of the conversation. "That's okay, Dad," he said. "We'll be all right." He covered the receiver with his hand and whispered to Leanne, "Can you stay a little longer? Dad has to work late." Leanne frowned. That would mean that the boys would be in bed when Bart came home, and she would have to face him alone. Taking a deep breath, she agreed. Excitedly Charlie spoke into the phone. "No Dad, she won't mind. She made a roast for supper. . . . Okay, we'll see you in the morning. Good night." Charlie dropped the receiver into its place, a broad grin on his face. "Why didn't you want Dad to know you were here? Did you want to surprise him?"

"Didn't you tell him?"

Charlie shook his head. "I thought you didn't want me to."

"So he thinks Mrs. Winters is staying with you. And why didn't you tell him Mathew was sick? He should know." Leanne tried not to sound harsh, but she was upset that Bart would come in unsuspectingly to find her there instead of his housekeeper.

"You sound like my mother already," Charlie said, grinning. "I wish you were, don't you?"

"Uh . . . let's finish the game and have dinner, Charlie." His question had shocked her, and she was relieved that he didn't push her to answer it.

Mathew slept through dinner, and afterward Charlie helped her put him to bed. Time passed slowly, and Leanne thumbed through magazines while Charlie watched television until his bedtime. After tucking him in, Leanne checked on Mathew and then settled herself on Bart's massive leather couch, burning the lamp on low. The less she could see of Bart's home, the easier it would be to forget where she was. But how could she forget? It was ridiculous even to try. She wondered what he would have thought if Charlie had told him she was there. After the cruel things she'd said the last time she saw him, she couldn't blame him if he never wanted to see her again. A glance at her watch told her it was nearly ten o'clock. Where could he be? She stifled a yawn before sliding her stockinged legs down the length of the couch. Carefully she pulled the skirt of her mint green sundress over her knees and rested her head against the arm of the couch.

"Leanne." She heard a voice calling her name, a soft whisper she barely recognized.

"Bart?" she asked sleepily, not able to open her heavy eyelids. She could feel him sitting next to her, his thigh near her arm. A warm hand moved over her bare shoulders, pushing the strands of silky hair away.

The distinct smell of musk filled her senses, and suddenly she was wide awake. She opened her eyes to see Bart's smiling gaze before he captured her open mouth.

Stiffening, Leanne pushed against him. "Bart," she whispered. "Let me go." Bart raised his head and looked down at her, a puzzled frown on his face.

"What is it, angel?" he asked, a twinkle in his eyes as he gently rubbed his thumb against the softness of her cheek.

Leanne swung her feet to the floor, giving herself leverage with which to push herself away from him. He moved, allowing her to stand. Her bare feet and mussed hair made her look like a small child. "What is it?" he asked again, moving toward her. She stepped back, extending her arm in front of her.

"Just leave me alone," she pleaded, ashamed of herself for letting him kiss her.

"What have I done? I come home feeling alone and depressed but find you lying here waiting for me, looking more beautiful than I remembered." He reached out and touched the fine strands of her hair, only to have her toss her head, throwing it back over her shoulder. "What did you want me to do?" he asked, shoving his hands into his trouser pockets.

Shaking, Leanne stuttered, "I don't know. I just didn't expect . . ." Frustrated, she pushed past him to look for her heels. "I've got to go," she said matter-of-factly, finding one shoe and putting it on. "The boys are asleep, and I left a plate of roast beef in the refrigerator for you."

Bart watched her frantically searching for the misplaced shoe as she stumbled around in only one heel. "Is this what you're looking for?" he asked, grabbing up the sandal from the edge of the couch and dangling it in front of her.

"Thank you," Leanne said, reaching for it, only to have him jerk it back. "That's not funny, Bart."

Bart tossed the shoe over his shoulder and grabbed her as she made for it. His mouth captured hers, and though her body stiffened and her lips were a thin, tight line, his gentle caresses burned through her defenses, making her blood run faster through her veins. It wasn't long before her arms betrayed her with the desperate need to hold him against her.

"Leanne," Bart groaned, his voice a hoarse whisper,

"it's been so long since I've loved or been loved. Help me to love again." Leanne's heart missed a beat. What was he saying? Did he love her and was just unable to say so? Did she dare hope? "I'm no good for you, Leanne, I know that, but you've been so good for me and I need you. Marry me, Leanne," he whispered, his face buried in the softness of her hair.

And Laura? Leanne thought, her body aching with the pain of knowing that Bart was capable of doing to Laura what Eric had done to her.

"I can't, Bart, I just can't," she cried, pulling away and snatching up her shoe, turning to face him, shoe in hand as if she meant to use it against him if she had to.

"You love me, Leanne. Admit it," he demanded, his hands on his hips.

"I don't!" she cried in confusion, shoving her foot into the shoe and picking up her purse. "I hate you. I hate you for ever coming into my life!"

"Then why are you here? What were you doing asleep on my couch if you weren't waiting for me? Your words say one thing, but your actions tell me something entirely different."

Shaking, Leanne stared at him in disbelief. He thought she had come to him. He had once told her to stay away from him if she didn't want him to touch her. Placing a hand to her flushed face, Leanne tried to calm herself. "I am not here for you, Bart," she said, holding her arms, her fingers digging into the flesh as she tried to control the nervous tremble that racked her body. "The school called me today. I came, Bart, because Mathew's sick, so don't flatter yourself." Turning from his shocked face, she jerked the door open and left, slamming it closed behind her.

Chapter Eleven

Leanne dated Stephen often during the next few weeks, making a conscious effort to forget Bart. It was over, and no amount of dreaming or crying would bring back the happy times she had shared with him. It was a fact she had to face, and so she threw herself into an active life where she wouldn't have time to think about the past.

Digging through her storage closet, Leanne pulled out an old, dusty bowling bag. Tugging on the rusty zipper, she finally was able to open it. She hadn't been bowling in at least two years and she'd been reluctant to accept Stephen's invitation to go this evening, but she was determined not to have idle time on her hands. Inside the bag, her bowling ball was still a shiny emerald green with mint-colored swirls. Placing her fingers in the holes, she stood and swung her arm back, getting the feel of the weight in her hands. She surprised herself by actually being excited. At one time she had been considered a pretty good bowler. "That was a long time ago," she reminded herself with a laugh, placing the ball between her feet on the floor so it wouldn't roll away. Pulling out an old pair of bowling shoes, she decided she would rather rent a pair tonight than wear the worn ones.

She wiped off the black bag and polished it until it looked new. No one would know it was the same one, she thought, admiring the job she had done. She threw the shoes in the trash and set the ball inside the bag along with a hand towel and a box of baby powder. All set, she thought. Dressed in jeans and a red calico shirt, she waited for Stephen on the redwood deck.

Fall had set in, and the trees made a colorful picture set against the orange-and-blue background of the sky. The evening was getting crisp, but Leanne pulled her jacket around her and ignored the shiver that ran up her spine. She remembered a day so long ago, when the air had been crisp and the fresh smell of spring had filled her lungs. Scanning the creek, she found the rock slab where she had fried fish for Bart and the boys. An emptiness crept inside her and she shook her head. She decided to wait for Stephen inside the house, where the memories weren't so vivid. Turning on a lamp, she picked up the Christmas-tree skirt she had been working on. She should have known better than to let herself sit and daydream—especially on the deck, facing the creek, of all places.

She had barely started a row of gold beads when she heard Stephen's car pull into the drive. Locking up the house, she went out to meet him. "You're late," she teased, climbing into the car.

"Not very." He laughed. "You must be really eager to go. Aren't you forgetting something?" he asked, looking in the direction of the house.

"What?" Leanne asked, puzzled. "Oh, yes. I guess it would be nice if I took my bowling ball," she said, spying her bag on the deck. Stephen jumped out of the car and got it for her, and they were on their way.

When they entered the bowling alley, the sound of pins flying and falling filled the room, creating an exciting atmosphere that Leanne had forgotten. She rented a pair of shoes, and Stephen led her to the alley he had taken. She was putting on her shoes while Stephen warmed up, getting a strike the first throw and a spare the next. He walked back toward her with a proud grin across his face.

"Looks like I'm going to have my work cut out for me," Leanne said, standing and sprinkling the baby powder on her hands. "You realize it has been at least two years since I've been bowling. Don't let that shiny bag fool you. I cleaned an inch of dust off it this afternoon." She laughed, picking up her ball and stepping onto the wooden platform. She lifted the ball and was preparing to take her first step when she realized that the woman in the lane next to her was about to bowl. Lowering her ball, Leanne waited for the woman to release her ball before she took her turn.

While she waited, she looked past the woman to a small boy who had his back to her. His honey-blond hair reminded her of Mathew, so she quickly turned her head. If it was Mathew, she didn't want to know. The woman hit a strike and Leanne drew her arm back, ready to release her ball, when Bart's laughter startled her. She dropped the ball with little control over it, causing it to roll halfway down the lane and into the gutter. Leanne knew now that the boy had been Mathew, and she purposely avoided looking in that direction when she walked back to the bench where Stephen was getting their score sheet ready.

"It has been a long time, hasn't it?" Stephen teased, mistaking the pain in her eyes for disappointment. "Don't worry, you'll get the hang of it again after you've thrown a few balls."

Leanne laughed halfheartedly. She didn't want to go up there again, but she knew she had to. She couldn't keep avoiding Bart. The possibility of running into him was great, and short of never coming into Tulsa again, she couldn't avoid it. When her ball came back, she steeled herself and, lifting the ball to her shoulder, stepped out on the platform. Concentrating on the pins at the other end, she sent the ball down the edge of the alley and watched with pride as it curved toward the center, knocking all but one of the pins down.

Stephen clapped his hands, causing Leanne to blush as she walked back to the rack. "It didn't take you long to catch on again, did it?" he asked. "I don't know if I should let you warm up anymore."

Unable to stop herself, Leanne glanced over toward Bart. He was standing next to Charlie, who was probably keeping score. His head was bent as he talked to his son, his hand on the back of Charlie's chair. Stephen followed her gaze and sighed. "Want to leave?" he asked, his voice low.

"No," Leanne said, turning to pick up her ball. "I'm

fine." She glanced again at Bart, then smiled at Stephen. "Let's see if I can get a strike this time," she said, her strength surprising him. Actually, it wasn't strength, she thought, sending the ball down the alley to claim only three pins. It was pride. She was tired of running from Bart.

She looked again in his direction while she waited for her ball to return. He was still talking to Charlie. Mathew balanced on one foot as he stood beside his father, trying to understand the complications of keeping score, which was apparently what Bart was trying to explain. Suddenly Leanne was staring into a pair of hazel eyes. They looked the same, yet somehow different. Trying to appear casual, she managed to smile. Bart said something to the boys, and they looked up and waved. Leanne lifted her hand, smiling, then turned away, unable to trust herself not to cry.

"It's your turn, isn't it, Stephen?" she asked, her voice shaky.

"Not really," Stephen said, coming to meet her. "But I'll finish yours."

"Thanks," she said, heading for the ladies' room, where she could cry unseen.

The restroom was empty, and, thankful for the privacy, Leanne leaned against a sink, her arms folded, her head bent. But the tears she expected never came. She just felt a numbness that she didn't understand. Did it mean she was over Bart? Hardly, she thought. "There is just no sense in crying," she said, turning to face her reflection in the mirror. Her eyes were too large and her cheekbones too hollow. She had lost weight in the last month. If she was going to keep up the pretense that she was over Bart, she would have to do something about her appearance. With the resolution to take better care of herself, she plastered a smile on her face and joined Stephen again.

It took great effort, but Leanne managed to finish two games without looking once in Bart's direction. Her scores were even gratifying. However, she didn't hesitate to agree with Stephen when he suggested they go to the drive-in down the street for hamburgers.

Leanne didn't get much sleep that night. She tossed and turned. Bart's face kept appearing in her dreams, his hazel eyes smiling, then narrowing in anger, before torturing her mouth with his kiss, a kiss she would never experience again. Waking before dawn, she recalled her dreams over hot coffee. He had seemed angry all the time. But why should *he* be? she thought. *I'm* the one who's been hurt . . . and used, she added in her thoughts.

Pouring her umpteenth cup of coffee, she shuffled down the hallway to the bathroom, where she prepared for work. After applying a scant amount of makeup, she slipped into gray wool slacks and a pink cashmere pullover sweater. The weatherman had predicted a cold front, and according to her outside thermometer in the kitchen window, he had been right.

In the office Leanne worked through the morning, going through a stack of reports on her desk. She had come in early, for lack of anything better to do, and was hoping to finish the stack by lunchtime. She heard her office door open, but she was too caught up in her report to look up.

"Surprise, surprise," a familiar voice said.

"Rhonda!" Leanne exclaimed, dropping the papers

on her desk and rushing to greet her cousin. "What are you doing in Tulsa? How long can you stay this time?"

"That's up to you," Rhonda said, tilting her head as she waited for Leanne to catch on to what she was saying.

"What do you mean? Are you staying with me?"

"Right now I'm staying with Mom and Dad, but if it's all right with you . . ."

"Of course you can stay with me. For as long as you want."

"You may be sorry you said that." Rhonda moved farther into the office, plopping down in a chair. "I've found what I was looking for in California, Leanne." Leanne settled on the edge of her desk, waiting for the rest of Rhonda's sentence, but all Rhonda did was smile teasingly.

"Well?" Leanne asked, impatiently.

"Can you go to lunch, or have you already been?"

Leanne threw up her hands in exasperation. "Will you please tell me what's going on?"

"Only if you let me buy you lunch."

"Oh, for heaven's sake!" Leanne said, reaching across her desk for her clutch bag. "Let's go."

They were crossing the hall toward the elevator when Stephen came out of his office. "Rhonda!" he exclaimed. "It's been a long time," he said, extending his hand.

"Hello, Stephen. It *has* been a long time. How have you been?" Rhonda took Stephen's hand, shaking it slowly. "I must say, you're looking good."

"Well, compliments I can handle. How about letting me buy you two some lunch at Chan's?"

Rhonda turned to Leanne for her opinion. "As long

as it doesn't stop you from telling me what your deep dark secret is."

Rhonda looked at Stephen. "It won't. After all, I'm among friends."

Rhonda insisted on taking her car, and since they couldn't all ride in Stephen's Jaguar, he and Leanne agreed. Rhonda pulled the silver Cougar onto the highway going the opposite direction from Chan's. Not the Paper Dragon again, Leanne thought.

"Rhonda, you're going the wrong way," Stephen said from the back seat. "Chan's is back there," he added, pointing his thumb over his shoulder.

"I remember," Rhonda said. "But I didn't think you'd mind if we stopped at my father's office before we ate."

Minutes later, Rhonda pulled off the highway into the parking lot of a high-rise office building. Parking the car near the entrance, Rhonda turned off the ignition key. "You two have to come with me," she said before getting out of the car and heading for the building.

Leanne looked from Rhonda to Stephen. "This must be it," she guessed, opening her door.

"Must be what?" Stephen asked, puzzled.

"Her secret. This has to do with her finding out something in California. I'm sure of it," Leanne explained, getting out of the car and waiting for Stephen. "Hurry," she said, rubbing her hands over her arms as the cold wind whipped around her. Stephen climbed out of the back seat and, putting an arm at Leanne's waist, ran along with her to the wide glass doors. Inside the lobby, they found Rhonda standing near the elevators, reading the roster. Leanne ran her fingers through her hair, trying to repair the damage the wind had done, while Stephen rubbed his hands together.

"It's really getting cold out there," he said, glancing up at the elevator signal. The arrow going up turned red and the doors opened. Leanne and Stephen moved to step inside, but Rhonda didn't join them, so they let the doors close without them. Leanne stood next to Rhonda, trying to figure out what she was looking at.

"There it is, Leanne," Rhonda said, a proud smile on her face.

Leanne searched the roster and finally found what she was looking for: Attorneys Holmes, Dempsey and Holmes. "Rhonda! How wonderful!"

"What's wonderful?" Stephen asked, still standing by the elevators.

"Uncle Ken has accepted Rhonda in his firm!"

"Hey, that's all right! Congratulations, Rhonda. That must have taken some doing," he said, admiringly. "I hear K. H. Holmes is the toughest criminal lawyer around."

"That's why I went to California. I had to prove to myself that I could be a success without my father's name behind me." Rhonda locked one arm in Stephen's and the other in Leanne's. "Come on, you guys. I'm starved."

That weekend, Stephen helped Rhonda move in with Leanne. "It's only temporary, I promise," she reminded Leanne. "My furniture is on its way, and I don't want to take an apartment without it."

"You've told me that a hundred times at least,"

Leanne teased as she carried an armful of hanging clothes up the redwood steps. "I hope you can find an apartment with enough closet space."

"I appreciate all this, really. I think I would have died if I had to stay at home another week."

"Couldn't you have left some of these clothes there for the time being?" Stephen asked, struggling with a trunk.

"Here, let me help you." Rhonda helped drag the trunk up the steps and into the living room. "I guess I could have left some of this mess, huh?"

Stephen and Leanne looked at each other and laughed. "Without them, you wouldn't be Rhonda," Leanne said, falling into a chair.

"So true," Stephen agreed as he placed an arm across Rhonda's shoulders. "But we wouldn't have you any other way."

Over the next few weeks Rhonda, Stephen and Leanne became a threesome, calling themselves the three musketeers. Leanne was thankful for Rhonda's crazy company. It helped to keep her mind off of Bart and allowed her no time for self-pity. Rhonda's furniture was lost, and it was after Thanksgiving before it was tracked down and she was able to move into an apartment of her own in town.

Leanne's small house seemed so quiet and empty after Rhonda left. But in the meantime, the Christmas season had crept up on her and she hadn't finished the tree skirt yet. Settling on the sofa, she picked up the needlework and began to stitch sequins and beads onto the felt material.

Rhonda and Stephen had invited her to go with them

to see the live nativity scene downtown, but she knew they would rather be alone and had declined, using the excuse that she would be taking her Sunday school class the next weekend. Stephen had been dating Rhonda seriously lately, and Leanne was happy for both of them. She had known that the time would come when she would have to give him time for his own life, and she was glad Rhonda was a part of it.

"Ouch!" Leanne jerked her hand. She had stabbed herself with the needle. Dropping the skirt onto the end table, she looked around the living room and sighed. She had moved all of her plants into the house to protect them from the cold, and still they seemed to droop. She recalled the day last spring when she had repotted most of them. The day she had nearly forced Stephen into driving so far on a date he knew nothing about. Smiling to herself, Leanne wondered why she had picked Tahlequah anyway. She could have just told Bart they were going to dinner or a movie. But then Bart wouldn't have had an excuse to go with them.

Looking back, she saw it all through different eyes. Bart had not only pursued her from the beginning, but he had been possessive, too, determined she wouldn't date Stephen. Why? she wondered, when he had had Laura all the while. Could he have ever *really* loved her, or any woman?

"Not much," she said to the walls, leaning forward to rest her elbows on her knees and her chin in her palms. But the way he held her in his arms, his kiss, his smile, all had seemed sincere. For a fleeting moment she wished she hadn't found out about Laura. What a fool I am, she thought. She would have eventually learned about Bart's involvement with the other woman.

Letting her head fall back, she stared at the ceiling, feeling lonely. "I can't just sit here feeling sorry for myself," she cried, jerking her head forward, pounding her fists on the sofa.

Determined to pull herself together, she walked into the kitchen, where she prepared a cup of hot chocolate. Putting on a holiday album, she settled at the table to write Christmas cards. The nativity scene decorated each one, and she felt a strong need to go to the live scene downtown. Maybe she would be able to regain the peace she had given up when she abandoned her prayer life for self-pity and doubt.

Leanne maneuvered her small car down the narrow strip of road between the parked vehicles on either side of her as she searched for a place to park. The turnout this year was tremendous, she thought, parking four blocks from the church. Bethlehem City, as the scene was called, had been created four years ago, and each year it had improved. Several churches pooled their efforts and built realistic booths out of used lumber, depicting various shops and an inn. The paved parking lot was strewn with hay, and characters dressed in biblical costumes roamed from shop to shop, pulling donkeys or carts laden with fruits, pans and bundles of cloth. A small, three-sided stable had been built at the end of the town, and Leanne especially enjoyed walking with the shepherds and wise men as they searched out the Christ Child.

The sound of Christmas carols could be heard from the steeple of the large old church, and Leanne was glad she had come. Her stereo certainly didn't compare to the beauty of church bells.

She was browsing through the true-to-life market-place when she heard a familiar voice call her. Turning, she saw Mathew running toward her, his face glowing as the cold wind whipped at his cheeks. Hugging him, she looked up, prepared to see Bart, but it was Laura who held Charlie's hand. A large, bearded man stood beside her with his arm across her shoulders.

"Hello, Leanne," Laura said. "This is my husband, Daryle."

"How do you do?" the man asked, extending a large gloved hand.

"Nice to meet you," Leanne said automatically, wondering if he knew about his wife and Bart.

"The boys have missed you. . . ." Laura went on, but Leanne was watching the man cross the walkway with Charlie and Mathew, showing them a stall with baby lambs. They must all be friends, Leanne thought.

"Bart misses you too, Leanne," the blond beauty said softly, gaining Leanne's full attention. "He's been a real mess since you stopped seeing him. He doesn't eat, he doesn't sleep, he's even stopped smoking and started going to church. He hasn't been this upset since Carol died."

Leanne was confused. "I don't understand," she said, pulling her coat up around her neck.

Laura studied Leanne's face. "I believe you really don't," she said. "But you should know that you put Bart in an awful spot. My sister's death was hard on us all, but Mother took it the worst. She clung to Mathew and Charlie as though they could take Carol's place. . . ."

Leanne's mind raced. "What? Are you Mathew and Charlie's aunt?"

"Yes, I am. Didn't you know that when you came to Bart's apartment that day?" The look on Leanne's face told her the answer. "Oh, my." She laughed. "You didn't think Bart and I . . . ? Oh, Leanne!" she said, hugging her. "You poor dear. What an unfortunate misunderstanding. I thought you were upset because I wanted to keep the boys. You see, Bart promised Mother and me that you wouldn't interfere with our relationship with the kids." Laura shook her pretty head. "Bart had left the night before . . ."

"But at the restaurant . . . the house you were going to decorate . . ."

"Daryle was out of town that night, and it was my birthday, so Bart and the boys took me out. And as for the house, Daryle and I just bought a home in the country this summer."

Leanne began to cry. She couldn't believe it. Bart had been sincere all along. He had wanted to marry her, but she had thrown those words of hate at him, walking out of his life.

Laura placed a warm arm over Leanne's shoulders and they walked. Leanne didn't care where they went. She had ached with pain before, but now she sobbed heavily with the knowledge that she had been her own undoing. Laura opened the large wooden door of the church, depositing Leanne inside the quiet sanctuary, leaving her there with only the whispered words, "Have faith."

The tall cathedral ceiling above her was dark. The only light came from the wall lamps along the side walls. Silently Leanne walked down the carpeted aisle, drawn to the front of the church by a large white cross surrounded by blue-and-red stained-glass windows. A white dove was pictured in the glass at the top right of the magnificent work of art.

There were people scattered throughout the large church, praying, giving thanks for the Christ Child, whose birthday grew near. Leanne had come to Bethlehem City every year since the community had first planned it. It was always a moving experience to walk among the shepherds and wise men making their way to the manger scene. Afterward, many people felt the need to visit the sanctuary for the quiet peace it offered.

Leanne slipped into a pew, feeling God's presence all around her compelling her to dry her tears and remember where she received her strength. She lifted her eyes toward the cross, silently praying that God forgive her for taking charge of her life and not trusting Him to handle it for her. What a mess I've made of things, she thought as more tears threatened to fall. Bart had been right that night when he accused her of cringing in a corner, afraid to love again, not trusting God to take care of her.

As she lowered her gaze she thought she saw Bart. Blinking the tears away, she looked again. It *was* Bart. He sat alone with his head in his hands, staring at the cold tiled floor at his feet. She was touched at seeing his strong, proud character now bent and humbled. Suddenly she realized the pain she must have caused him, shutting him out of her life without even an explanation. If only she could go to him, to explain. Maybe he could forgive her. But Bart was a man who held grudges, she thought, recalling how he was unable to forgive Stephen or even himself. No, she had caused him enough pain. It would be best if she simply left before he saw her. As if he sensed her watching him, Bart lifted his dark head and stared at her, a blank look on his face.

She had waited too long to slip out unseen, but she averted her gaze and stepped into the aisle anyway. She had to leave. It hurt too much to know she had had his love but had thrown it away. Her eyes were full of tears as she walked slowly toward the entrance. He had once thought she was an angel, but now he must think she had been sent by Lucifer himself, for all she had done was cause him pain.

Scenes from the past months flooded her thoughts. The confrontation at the airport and again in Stephen's office. She had even said she hated him. How could he think she would be jealous of the boys and their aunt? Why didn't someone tell her? Why couldn't he see she was jealous of him? Leanne clenched her fists at her side. She was hurt and angry—angry with herself for never telling Bart she loved him. She should have fought for him. If only she had trusted him, and trusted God.

When she reached the last pew, she turned to look at Bart once more, but he wasn't where she had last seen him. He was in the aisle only a few pews behind her. His hazel eyes held hers, and though she knew she should leave, she stayed, watching him come toward her.

Bart seized her arms and pulled her into the isolation of a nearby alcove.

"I'm sorry, Bart. I'm so sorry," she cried before he could turn his anger on her.

"Please, Leanne, listen to me. We've wasted so much time already," he pleaded with her anxiously. "I had promised myself to stay out of your life, but without you my world was so empty. I had to fill it with something . . . but there was nothing. Then I remembered what you had said about God taking an impossible situation and making it right. So I prayed. I've prayed for so long, Leanne. I can't make you love me, only God can do that. But I do love you and I want you to trust me and be my wife."

Leanne's eyes grew wide, the tears of pain replaced by drops of joy that fell down her cheeks freely. She saw the sincerity in his eyes as they searched hers. "Bart . . ." she began, then watched his hazel eyes as he waited intently for her answer. His eyes revealed the warmth of a man who knew love. "I do trust you, Bart, and I love you. I love you so very much."

"I knew it," he said before his kiss rushed life back into her numbed senses.

Slowly she moved into the circle of his arms, placing her small hands behind his head, drawing his face close to hers. "I've been such a fool, Bart."

"Marry me," he whispered, his breath warm on her face as he ignored her words. His lips touched hers tenderly; then he studied her face, anxious for an answer.

"First I have to explain—"

"Explain?" he whispered hoarsely. "Even you, my sweet angel, can't explain how only minutes ago I prayed to God that He would bring you back into my life, and here you are in my arms, an answer to a humble prayer."

"Then you forgive me?" she whispered, breathlessly.

"Anything!" he murmured, his forehead resting against hers. "You've taught me to love and to trust

God. He has taught me to forgive—even to forgive myself," he added as he moved to see her face. *"Now will you answer me?"*

"Yes, Bart. Oh yes!"

Like a fire kindled by trust, their passion grew and hungrily Bart tasted the sweetness of her mouth. Leanne thought her lungs would burst when, reluctantly, he drew back to gaze at her and she saw the joyful smile in his hazel eyes, a smile that she knew was hers alone.